# Eclectic
# Moments

Vanessa J. Horn

Printed in the United Kingdom

First Printing, 2015 Alfie Dog Limited

The author can be found at: authors@alfiedog.com


ISBN 978-1-909894-27-3


Published by
**Alfie Dog Limited**
Schilde Lodge, Tholthorpe,
North Yorkshire, YO61 1SN
Tel: 0207 193 33 90

# DEDICATION

To Mum with all my love and gratitude for
everything you have done for me; I know how proud
you would have been to see my book in print.

# CONTENTS

# ACKNOWLEDGMENTS
*(In alphabetical order)*

Thanks, Bigger, for always being proud of whatever I do and dragging me out for cake outings when necessary (not that I actually *needed* much dragging…) By the way, yes I *do* expect you to read this book!

Koff, thanks for providing the title for the collection and giving me your down-to-earth Northern viewpoint whenever my writing threatened to become too fanciful!

Thanks, Loz, for all the lovely times when you, me and Nanny played sisters and air hostesses, drew, painted and made things together. Thanks for being you.

Thanks to Nix and Scoobs for all the hilarious occasions when we made up dances and recorded videos of each other prancing around the living room.

Thanks, Steph, for proof-reading and critiquing so many of my stories and for encouraging me to get them published rather than continuing to write even more (if it weren't for you, I'd probably still be churning them out without a thought of publishing them!)

Tubs, thanks for all your support during my sabbatical year.

# 1
# WHAT'S IN A NAME?

It was very sudden, I'll grant you that; one moment I was staring out of the office window, calculating how many more minutes until I could nip out for my ciggie break and the next… well, to put it bluntly, I was dying.

Initially, when the mist had begun to swirl around me, I'd thought – as would be perfectly natural on a Friday morning – I was just daydreaming. Albeit very realistically. After all, I wasn't expecting death; I wasn't ill, involved in an accident or even that old. However, a small clue quickly emerged when the pastel-type haze was quickly followed by short cinematic-type excerpts. Of my life. The good bits, the bad bits, even the mediocre bits.

By then, of course, I knew I was in trouble – I mean, we've all heard about those moments just before death, when your life is projected before you. In order for you to take stock, I suppose. So now it was just a question of waiting for the bright light and guardian angel to appear and that was me. Done.

Not that I wasn't annoyed about this occurrence – don't get me wrong, I'm no saint. If I'd had time to gather my thoughts rationally, I'd definitely have been peeved that I was dying way before I was ready (although, admittedly, I suppose most people *would* say that). Equally, I'd have berated myself at my lack of achievement in life; the things I hadn't done, hadn't said, hadn't realised. As I said, though, it was all happening so fast. Too fast.

Anyhow, before I could even blink, there he was: my guardian angel! Or so I assumed - he being the only person travelling towards me on a strong beam of radiance with his arms outstretched. Wide smile on his face. Although he was rather shabbily clothed, to be truthful - not quite what you'd expect. Man at Oxfam I'd have described him, if pushed to do so. Still, it didn't do to be too picky about these things; I myself was not the sharpest dresser, at work or in my social circle. Good clothes didn't necessarily maketh the man, after all.

Before I could so much as pose a question, or even comment on this turn of events, the slightly dishevelled – angel? - grabbed my hand and quickly led me into the beam of light. Whereupon we were whizzed upwards, and innerwards too, if that makes sense. Next thing I knew, we were standing outside an impressive pair of golden gates surrounded by whirling clouds and mists of sorbet-delicious colours. In front of this entrance was an elderly man, sporting a long beard and carrying a bejewelled clipboard. All rather clichéd, I felt at this point, and still incredibly dream-like. I wouldn't have been surprised if I'd blinked and suddenly found myself back at the office, still staring out of the window. But I didn't. Couldn't.

The older man peered at me curiously, from head to toe. Then slowly shook his head. Frowning deeply, he turned to address my scruffy companion, his voice low and resonating. "He's not expected."

Now I was the one to frown (though probably not so impressively). I too turned to my scruffy companion – now to be referred to as SC. My voice came out shakily and at least a semitone higher than normal. "What does he mean, *not expected?*"

At this point, SC was shifting nervously from foot to foot, turning an unfetching shade of cerise. Ignoring me, he spoke to the other man first. "But I went to the correct place, sir, followed all the rules like you're supposed to – he *is* the right one: Drake Barton!"

The older man let out an elongated groan, slapping the side of his head noisily with his palm. "No! You fool, you were supposed to fetch Blake Downton! *Blake Downton!*"

SC blinked and then shuddered, seeming to grow smaller by the second while we stared at him accusingly. Muttering something that sounded a little like "Bloody dyslexia!" he turned away from us, giving one of the golden gates a hefty kick. I'm assuming it was solid gold, for all the impact he made on it. After yelling and hopping around in pain for a few moments, he finally collapsed onto the ground in an untidy heap.

Shaking my head in bewilderment, I addressed the elderly man. "So it's a mistake, then? I wasn't supposed to die today? I can go back?"

He looked downwards. Sighed, rather protractedly, it seemed. His voice was considerably softer now. "Yes, yes and, regrettably… *no*."

I processed this information relatively quickly (for me) "No I can't go back? Why not, if I shouldn't have been brought here in the first place?"

Now he looked up, his eyes meeting mine. Eyes of deep brown, tinged with rings of black. I thought I could detect some sympathy in his expression. Or empathy, at least. "I'm afraid once you've travelled through, the way back is sealed. For ever. You will just have to wait now until it's your time to enter."

Could this really be correct? "But when *is* my time to

enter?" I was feeling more than a little anxious now, to be perfectly truthful. I've never been renowned for my patience, and there didn't seem to be a lot of action going on here. If I had to stay around for too long, I was in danger of becoming incredibly bored.

The elderly man (EM) consulted his clipboard list. Turned over a page. And another. Finally, after what seemed like an eternity of rustling sheets, he sighed then mumbled his reply: "September 2nd 2035."

"What? *What?* I'm not hanging around for" – I made a rapid calculation – "over twenty years!" I threw another accusing scowl at SC who was now resting against the gates, carefully inspecting his injured toes.

Reddening once again, he muttered, "Sorry," and then, seemingly devoid of any verbal expansion, returned his gaze to his foot.

I rolled my eyes heavenwards – obviously now closer than it had been this time yesterday, albeit still inaccessible – and addressed EM again. "What do you suggest I do while I wait?" I was trying to stay polite; nevertheless, I could hear a querulousness in my voice – but then that was surely understandable in the circumstances.

EM was considering. Scratching his beard thoughtfully. "Legislation states - not that this type of misfortune occurs very often, of course – that you are not permitted to 'hang around', as you put it. Not by yourself, anyway. Therefore, you will need supervising until such time as you can legally enter Heaven. Given that it was one individual – and one individual only - that put you in this unfortunate position, it would seem reasonable that he should be your appointed custodian during this time."

SC and I exchanged dubious glances; neither of us

looked exactly thrilled at the idea.

Disregarding the hostile vibes, EM walked over to SC. Tugged him ungently to his feet and spoke firmly. "If you carry out this mission successfully then you *may* be considered eligible to continue in your position of Retriever. Eventually. Providing you also undertake some additional training for your reading problems, of course."

SC sighed, seemingly unimpressed. Exhaled deeply. Ultimately, possibly having weighed up his options and finding them limited, he shrugged and turned to me. Placed a hand on my shoulder and led me away from EM and the golden gates. "Come on then."

***

As we strolled away, through the mists of colours and haze, I glanced at my newly-appointed guardian. He hadn't uttered a word since our departure from the golden gates, and was seemingly deep in thought. I cleared my throat noisily. "So, what now? Where are we supposed to go for two decades?"

Suddenly grinning, SC drew me closer. "Right. Now, don't get too excited, but I think I know of someone who can help get you into Heaven before your time."

I looked at him dubiously. Far from being excited, I couldn't help wondering if this was going to be yet another mess-up.

My reserve must have been obvious, for SC puffed out his cheeks indignantly, frowning. "Look, it's got nothing to do with reading, ok?"

I considered. Nodded slowly – what did I have to lose? "Alright, let's do it."

***

There was something about this place that made it impossible to identify how much time had passed; it could've been minutes or even hours since we set off, but at some point we reached a clearing in the vapours. SC brought us to a halt. "Here."

I looked around curiously, but before I had time to comment, I spotted a dark shape looming out of the mist. "The Accelerator," SC whispered.

A large male figure stood before us. Of indeterminate age, dark-complexioned features and sporting an impressively well-developed body, he was the kind of man you didn't want to get on the wrong side of. Ever. He raised a bushy eyebrow. "Yes?" His voice was unsurprisingly deep, matching his physique and demeanour perfectly.

Nervously, SC explained our predicament, glossing over his own failings in the erroneous scenario. He wittered on for some time before concluding breathlessly, "So we need to get Blake – um, Drake - into Heaven as soon as possible."

The Accelerator was silent for a few moments whilst studying us both. Then he replied. "And if I were to... *help* you with this dilemma, what would you be able to offer me in return?"

SC shrugged, holding out his hands. Empty. Without a lot of optimism, I delved into my trouser pockets: a packet of chewing gum, 97p and – unexpectedly - a small ball bearing. Being whisked away without time to throw my jacket on was obviously not to my advantage.

I blurted out, "Maybe there's something I can *do* for you instead – a favour of some sort?"

His voice was gruff now. "A *favour?*"

"Yes – anything," I cringed, not usually one to beg, but equally not often found in this bizarre type of situation. Desperate measures and all that...

The Accelerator considered my appeal, looking me up and down as if to determine what use I could possibly be to him. Eventually, an idea seemed to occur to him. He pursed his lips in – I hoped – an approximation of a smile. "Well… I suppose as you are relatively fresh, it *would* mean you have an advantage; you'd be able to access certain areas that I cannot. Areas such as the Edge…"

There was a sudden gasp from SC, indicating that this errand was evidently not going to be an agreeable one. But I remained silent, waiting for the Accelerator to continue. Wanted to find out more before I made my decision.

Possibly encouraged by a lack of immediate refusal, the Accelerator moved closer, now even taking one of my hands in his. "The Edge is the hairline precipice between life and death. Although you can't step back to Earth, from there you gain a view of the goings-on – can observe friends, relatives back on Earth. I need to find out how my family are coping without me, two years on… If you could just get close enough to see that they are in good form, it would bring me considerable peace of mind."

I thought about his request. "If I travel to this *Edge* - is it dangerous?" As I said the words, I couldn't help feeling a bit foolish; after all, I was *dead* – what worse fate could befall me, after all?

The Accelerator bit his lip. Heaved a sigh. "There is a *slight* risk of being lost between the two civilisations, but that's only if you go too close to Earth; if you're vigilant, you'll have no problem. At all. However, if you're careless, well…"

Beside me, SC shuddered, whispering, "You don't want to know."

And actually I didn't. I already knew that I was going

to undertake this mission, dangerous or not. For, basically, there was no way I was going to wander around in the mists for twenty years, waiting for my legal entrance to Heaven. I nodded at the Accelerator. "I'll do it!"

***

Surprisingly, as I followed the swirling path that I'd been directed to, I felt no nerves, no fears. Rather, I was gratified that, finally, I had something purposeful to do. Something constructive. I increased my pace, ignoring SC dragging his heels in my wake. Eventually, I was aware of him sitting down behind me with a noisy grunt. "This is as far as I can go," he said, with obvious relief. "I'll wait for you here."

Nodding my assent, I continued on my way, observing that the coloured haze around me was now thickening and making it difficult to see very far ahead. For the first time since leaving the Accelerator, I experienced a slight unease; how would I know when I reached the Edge – would it be obvious where to stop or would I accidentally blunder on and fall over the precipice? And even if I didn't, would I be able to recognise the Accelerator's family in order to report back to him successfully? So many doubts. But, despite my anxieties, I kept walking. What else could I do?

Eventually, I spotted a thin contour of land in front. Was that it? Had I reached the Edge? My heart fluttered; could I really be so close to Earth; to my former life, my former self? I hurried towards the solid-seeming strip, all the while keeping aware of my footfalls, anxious not to cross the invisible but lethal line which would render me misplaced. As I grew closer, I slowed down - took even more care. And yes, I could now see how thin the Edge actually was; one step too far and you *would* be lost. I stopped still and peered down at the void which separated the two civilisations; I could see nothing but blackness down there, although - when I listened carefully - I was aware of a faint howling sound. Lost souls? Demons? I didn't care to find out – I needed to get on with my mission and achieve my goal.

Averting my eyes from the deep chasm, I gazed instead across at Earth. Although it was recognisable *as* Earth, I didn't perceive it in the same way as when I'd existed there. For a start, as my eyes travelled across the land, it seemed, initially, just as a whirling juxtaposition of freeze-frame scenarios. Then, when I concentrated on any particular region, the people and objects in that zone would immediately become animated, seemingly going about their daily lives. I could even make out features, expressions. Hear their comments, observations. Incredible! After zooming in and out for a while, I comprehended that what I would need to do was to scan along systematically until I located the Accelerator's family – whoever and wherever they might be - then focus in to obtain details and specifics of what they were doing. Right...

As I've mentioned before, time travels differently here. Certainly not in minutes and hours, as far as I can tell. So all I know is that after a specific period, my eyes began to feel tired with straining, my soul dispirited with disappointment. After all, I didn't really know who I was looking for so how could I possibly know when I found them?

Suddenly, my fevered concentration was startled by a noise behind. Quickly turning round, I was surprised to see SC nervously approaching me. Unexpectedly pleased to see him, I was nevertheless uneasy that he had come this far. "I thought you couldn't –"

He nodded quickly, his eyes flicking nervously towards the Edge. "I know – it's highly irregular, not to mention dangerous - but I felt guilty about letting you go alone; it's my fault you're in this predicament, after all. My conscience told me I had to come and help."

I glanced at his face; he was sweating profusely but seemed to have a previously unseen determination. I was quite impressed, despite my previous lack of faith in him. "Thanks… but just be careful you don't get too close. Have you any idea what I'm looking for here?"

He nodded again, his eyes peering anxiously over the edge of the precipice. "Yes, that's why I came; I'm one of the team who collected the Accelerator – not that he was called that then – and I've seen his family, have an idea where they can be located." He saw me glance at him knowingly. He blushed a little. "And before you say anything, no I didn't get that one wrong!"

I raised my eyebrows resignedly. Just me then. Anyway, I suppose it didn't matter that much now – it was too late to change things *and* we had a job to accomplish. "Ok, let's get this done.

SC proved invaluable, obviously. I don't know how long I'd have had to stay at the Edge, scanning frantically until I got some kind of clue as to who I was looking for, but with him there, at least I had some kind of an advantage. And, as if to prove my point, pretty soon he gave a small exclamation. Pointed downwards. "There – that's them!"

I stared curiously in the direction of his finger. Yes, I couldn't mistake the dark swarthiness that marked this family out as belonging to the Accelerator. A middle-aged woman, two adult sons… ok, well, they looked happy enough. Healthy. Going about their daily lives. But… who was this with them - this tall blond man? They seemed quite fond of him. I frowned, wondering if he was another member of the family. A distant cousin, maybe? SC and I exchanged glances. He shrugged but indicated that we should tune in – gain more information. As we listened and watched, it became apparent that the Accelerator's wife had done more than just survive since her husband had died; she'd obviously set up a new life for herself with a new man. Okaay…

Simultaneously, SC and I averted our eyes away from the family. Moved back from the Edge and sat a safe distance away. We contemplated silently then, finally, spoke at the same time:

"Do you think I should –?"

"What will you –?"

Our combined laughter broke the uneasy atmosphere. Echoed all around the dispiriting place which was the Edge, and drifted way up high into the surrounding coloured mist.

SC shot me a quick glance. "I'd heard the Accelerator was quite a villain in his time, you know. A good family man, yes, but underhand in his business dealings. Apparently."

I didn't find that hard to believe. "I suppose the very fact that, even here, he's running an underhand service doesn't commend him highly. Still…" Being a good family man *was* a strong redeeming feature. But was it enough? And, of course, the truth was that I needed him, flaws or not. So I needed to make a decision.

SC was watching me anxiously. "I think we need to go back." He was obviously keen to return to the comparative safety of the mists.

I chewed my lip thoughtfully. "Yeah, we've seen all we need to. Now."

***

As we strolled back through the haze, my mind was whirling as much as the mists around us. I thought about what we'd witnessed. Mulled over my predicament. Considered lies, truths, white-lies and compromises. I still had no idea exactly what I would tell the Accelerator; I could only hope that the right thing would come to me. Eventually.

The density lessening the further we walked, I became more aware of my surroundings. Either I was becoming used to being here, or the whole experience was sharpening my senses. Now I could see the vapours not just as a swirling mass but rather as separate patterns, meanderings, configurations. I wondered if each one had a symbolism of a sort. Or perhaps they were forms of landmarks, directing individuals like a 3D map. It was possible, I supposed. Not that we had seen anyone, of course, either journeying to or from the Edge. Although that was probably because of the risky nature of the area. After all, who knew what type of calamity could transpire out here?

Soon, from a distance up high, and seemingly deceptively small because of this, I could see the Accelerator watching our return. He came swiftly towards us, his expression anxious. Apprehensive. *A good family man*. Gradually, my doubts floated up to the surface of my consciousness and then dispersed. Taking a deep breath, I began to speak. Decisively. Assuredly. "I saw them. All is well – you have nothing to worry about." Slowly, the Accelerator's expression relaxed until his cheeks were smooth and his lips formed a broad smile.

He clasped both of my hands in his. Surprisingly, his grip was warm. Reassuring, even. "Thank you so much; this means a great deal to me."

I nodded; I'd done the right thing. There would have been no point in telling him of the interloper who had taken his place - what good could it possibly have done? No, he was definitely best not knowing. I looked up into his eyes. "I've kept my side of the bargain – now I'd like you to help me to get into Heaven. Please?"

The Accelerator bowed, a formal gesture which seemed appropriate somehow, in the circumstances. He pointed towards a ray of light behind him. I did a double-take; I'm sure that shaft of light hadn't been there previously – we'd have definitely seen something like that amidst all the swirls and mists; it would have stood out like the proverbial sore thumb. I looked again. If I squinted, I could just about make out a small silver gate at the end of the beam. The Accelerator cleared his throat. "It's the back gate to Heaven."

I continued to scrutinise the access. Frowned. "It looks to be guarded – I can see someone sitting beside it?"

The Accelerator nodded. "The caretaker, yes. That's the only problem to overcome."

SC snorted suddenly. "Quite a big problem, I'd say. I thought you were going to get Drake straight into Heaven – no more obstacles?" He folded his arms and stared defiantly at the other man.

I, in turn, stared at him; this scruffy companion of mine seemed ever-surprising; I didn't know he had it in him to speak to someone like the Accelerator like that. I shook my head disbelievingly.

Unexpectedly, the Accelerator laughed, the deep noise cutting through the vapours around us, seeming to clear a pathway directly to the back gate. Now this option seemed more manageable – apart from the guard, of course. Without the mists, I could see… *her* more clearly. "It's a woman," I whispered to SC.

He peered over at her and then whispered back to me. "Seems to be, yes."

Having fulfilled his promise – in *his* view - The Accelerator seemed ready to leave. "It's up to you now – I've shown you the way in; all you have to do is take it." With a sonorous chuckle, he strode away, back into the haze.

I stared after his retreating back. Muttered, "Thanks for nothing." Then turned to SC. "That's it then – we're scuppered."

SC frowned. "Hey, my friend; no reason to give up at this stage." He placed a conciliatory arm around my shoulders. "Look at it this way, we just have one more obstacle to face. Just one, that's all. A woman."

I shook myself free from his rather suffocating embrace. "Yes – a woman. One of those creatures that I've had absolutely no success with in the whole of my life. What makes you think things are going to be so different in my death, hmm?"

"Aha – you might not have been a lady's man but I," - and here SC puffed out his chest with some self-satisfaction – "*I* was quite the player of my time. Yes, with my beguiling ways and charm, I'll have you into Heaven in no time. In fact, in less than no time. Just you see."

I frowned. A *lady's man* – SC? It seemed unlikely. However, in the grand scheme of things, it may not have been the most unlikely manifestation since I came here. I sighed. Once again, I was putting myself in his hands, but, once again, there was no option. "Come on then,

14

Lothario."

As we strolled along the ray, towards the bright silver gate, I couldn't help but feel the smallest tinge of excitement. Was I finally going to gain entry to Heaven, with all its glory and goodness? Was this it? However, as we drew closer to the silver gate, the expression on the elderly woman's face became clear. She didn't look happy. She didn't look happy at all. My spirits dropped as quickly as they had risen. Another setback?

She addressed SC harshly. "What is it? What do you want?"

SC paled a little and then rallied round. "Now then, that's no way to treat a couple of travellers. We've come from far and wide just to visit you, you know."

I frowned. That was a bit over the top, surely?

The woman obviously thought so too. "Far and wide my serpent! What you want is easy access to Heaven, am I right?"

SC hesitated, then changed his tone to one he probably imagined was alluring. Charming, even. "Well, that would be very pleasant, naturally, but for the while, we are quite happy to stand here and converse with you."

The woman wasn't convinced. She grunted loudly. "As if."

Defeated, I turned to SC. "Let's go – we're just wasting our time here. We'll have to look for some other way."

Unpredictably, the caretaker reached out and took my arm. "Not so quick, sunshine. I didn't refuse *you* entry. Only your haphazard friend here. *You*, on the other hand, are quite welcome to enter." The caretaker shrugged. "In actual fact, I had every intention of letting you in. With those baby blues, who could resist?" She smiled a toothless grin at me and I realised that my luck had probably not changed.

I blinked rapidly, and then levelled a quick glance at SC. He grinned back at me, seemingly unperturbed. Giving me the thumbs up, he then turned round to leave, clicking his heels in the air in celebratory manner. After watching him retreat for a few moments, I took a deep breath and began to walk slowly through the opened silver gate.

# 2
# COMMITTED

I stare out of the finger-smudged window. Rain lashes down relentlessly; driving sheets of water punctuated only by the mountainous masses in the distance. Hillocks of waste matter. Waste matter that is practically ignored by Aberfan residents though; for familiarity breeds contempt, as the saying goes.

I turn my attention back to the twenty-three children at their desks. Some are still staring at their sums in bemusement, while others speedily scratch with fat-leaded pencils in hope of being first to finish. I smile.

My first class. It seems much longer than eight weeks since I first entered this room, suddenly elevated from student to teacher, after four years of training. A class of my own. Exciting. Exhilarating. Oh, and exhausting too, of course…

I stifle a yawn and remind myself – not that I need much reminding - of next week. Half-term. Much as I've enjoyed these past two months, I'm looking forward to a week with no marking, no still stiffly-uncomfortable suit to put on every morning and no alarm clock waking me at the crack of dawn. So… one day to go.

"Sir, sir!" Johnny Evans, of course. He can't survive for more than ten minutes without a morsel – however insignificant – of attention. He's bouncing around in his chair now like an over-active puppy desperate to be let outside. Arms flailing, he knocks Susan Hughes's felt pencil-case to the floor. She rolls her eyes as she swiftly retrieves it, now placing it out of his reach. Susan has three small brothers at home; maybe it's a bit much to insist that she shares a desk with yet another lad at school. The thing is, though, she's a great calming influence on the boisterous Johnny...

"Yes, Johnny – what is it?" I answer him quickly now before he can cause any more chaos in our small classroom.

"Sir, it's just that I was wondering if we'd get out to break today. We've had to stop in for three days now, and me and me mates want to play footie!" He affects an anxious expression, opening his blue eyes wide in, I assume, an attempt to win me over. As if I control the weather.

I cast another look through the window, observing that, if anything, the rain is even heavier now. And the mist is closing in like ominously suffocating cotton-wool, swathing the slagheaps in an eerie murkiness. I shiver.

Turning back to the small boy in front of me, I shake my head reluctantly. "No, I don't think so, Johnny. It doesn't look as if this rain's stopping any time soon."

Johnny's lips pull downwards and there's a ripple of discontent around the classroom. As the muttering escalates, sounding increasingly like a group of irate wasps buzzing around unwelcoming blooms, I hurriedly devise a compromise. "Look, if it stops raining by this afternoon, we'll go out for a run around – how does that sound?"

But any response I might have had is suddenly obliterated by a strange reverberation from outside. Roaring? Rumbling? I frown, unable to identify the noise. A jet? It could be, I suppose, although we don't get many over this part of Wales; just the occasional light plane, that's all. Yet I can't imagine what else it could be. And it's loud: very loud. The children look up at the window curiously and then turn their puzzled eyes to me, needing clarification. Reassurance.

I feel myself frowning as the noise grows ever louder and closer. Now thunderous. Like liquid gravel advancing and surging. Grating and corroding. Not a jet then. Some sort of attack? A bomb? With vague childhood memories of the war, I suddenly recall being ushered to take refuge under the stairs at home during a raid. I shout, "Get under your desks!" to my confused class. But they have no time - darkness suddenly blankets the gloomy daylight as dirty sludge begins to slide under the door. A black bulk. Infiltrating our classroom, it swells and spreads in confidence and quantity with total disregard for property or life. We stare, stunned, as the thick mass engulfs chairs, desks, equipment…

Screaming? There must be, but I hear nothing other than the thundering quagmire as it surges into the room, filling every nook, every crevice. Panicking, I push back my chair to rise, but immediately lose my footing as the mud and rubble shoves and distorts around me. Fear. Frustration. I need to be in control - I need to protect and shield the children. I reach out, desperately trying to grab at flailing arms, kicking legs, but the stinking mass overpowers and diminishes like tainted treacle, greasily slicking my hands and fingers into vulnerability. Children slip away from me as easily as dandelion fluff blowing over a hedge. I'm powerless.

From the partially submerged floor, I turn my head this way and that, desperately trying to find a solution, only half-registering the heaving collection of books, pencils and other learning paraphernalia which are merging together in a surreal educational stew. The mass is rapidly rising; I see it in sharp-edged clarity, almost as if in slow motion, but in actuality it's only taking milliseconds to overwhelm and overpower. Suddenly - a sharp blow to the back of my head - a chair? A table? Then… oblivion.

\*\*\*

I come to with the sensation of over-tight blankets crushing my limbs. I'm compressed. Compacted in blackness. I squint. No flicker of light, no glimmer of life. Just a tiny pocket of air in which to breathe. I spread my fingers further out into the encompassing sludge, feeling out for anything… *anyone*.

Something hard – a book? I keep pushing. Then, eventually… a softness… A child? I reach for a hand. Press gently. Nothing. I squeeze again. This time I'm rewarded with a tiny movement. Life!

I close my eyes in relief, still clutching this delicate link to humanity. Johnny? Susan? Evan? It doesn't matter who it is – I just know I mustn't let go. So I hold on. And wait…

*Any similarity to names of those involved in the disaster is purely coincidental. Although based on real events this story is an entirely fictional account.*

# 3
# THE BUTTERFLY

Toby held his breath as he shuffled forward on his stomach, net in hand. Almost there. Centimetre by centimetre, second by second. He paused. Watched as the large Red Admiral fluttered unsteadily above the buddleia bush, and then came to rest on one of the lilac-purple blossoms. Settled, wings outstretched. Now. Hands shaking slightly, he raised his net and manoeuvred it carefully towards the butterfly. Slowly. Steadily. But he was a heartbeat too late; the butterfly startled and rose just before the net made contact, trembling upwards in search of safer pastures.

Toby sighed heavily and rolled over onto his back, gazing up at the sky and the tiny speck which was the departing butterfly. He'd come close that time: *so* close to getting his first butterfly. Close but not close enough. He frowned and gnawed gently at his ragged thumb nail. For five whole weeks now he'd been trying – *ages* – and still he had no butterflies. He just *had* to get them soon, before the holidays were over. He *needed* them.

His passion had begun just before the end of a long and hot summer term. At the end of one particularly humid afternoon, Mrs Holland had taken her Year 3 class outside under the shady trees to read them a story: 'Butterfly Summer'. Sitting next to his teacher, Toby had listened in rapture; been captivated by the idea of the butterfly garden described in the tale. Smells and sounds of school had faded into obscurity as her words transported him into wonder and magic. Safe. Secure.

Later, after school, he'd thought about the story some more. Had realised that it was exactly what he and Mum and Alex needed: a special butterfly place. He'd wrinkled his nose, trying to think what Mrs Holland had called it. Sank something… No, sanktu - *sanctuary*, he'd smiled, remembering. So that had become his goal – to bring together their guardian butterflies in his garden. Create their own sanctuary. But it had been much harder than he'd thought; he'd yet to collect even one butterfly in three whole weeks of trying. Not one.

The sound of raised voices from indoors brought him abruptly back to the present. The same old things being shouted: something about 'gap year' from Alex and then 'university' from Mum – words that seemed to have been repeated again and again for months now. Toby could never make much sense of the arguments, but he did know that if he could make his butterfly garden then everything would be ok. He needed to keep trying. With renewed enthusiasm, he picked up the net and ventured towards the wild section at the end of the garden. Mum hadn't had any time to weed that area yet: surely there'd be loads of butterflies there.

Pushing through the knee-high grasses, Toby came to a sudden halt as he spotted an animated yellow shape on a bush ahead. He drew the net warily from behind him and tip-toed closer. Closer still. The little butterfly didn't seem to have noticed him; was busy fluttering from leaf to leaf. When he was near enough, Toby slowly eased the net over the bush, using tiny, smooth movements. Closer. Closer. Until… Success – the butterfly was in the net! He closed his eyes briefly and let out a long drawn-out but soft, "Yesssss." At last – he'd done it.

Gently, he scooped the butterfly from the bush, taking care to place his hands underneath the net so she wouldn't escape. He carried her back up the garden until he reached the steps, then finally - sitting down with the net in his lap - allowed himself a good look at his treasure. The butterfly looked even smaller now than she had on the bush; she had drawn her wings up tightly and was trembling against the mesh. Toby's excited smile faded. Bringing his face close to the butterfly, he whispered to it softly, like he'd seen their next-door neighbour comfort her baby. "There, there, pretty butterfly, there, there…" But the butterfly trembled even more, tucking her face into her body as if she were trying not to be there. A tiny shivering ball of yellow.

Toby sat back on his haunches, confused. It wasn't supposed to be like this. All the butterflies in the story were glowing in happiness and confidence; not scared, like this one. Why was his butterfly different? Staring upwards – bewildered - his attention was caught by another butterfly hovering across the garden. Wings outstretched, the butterfly seemed to be smiling in the sunlight, free to choose where and when she flew. Toby looked back down to his butterfly in the net, then up at the airborne butterfly. A heavy, dark feeling flooded over him.

In a split-second-made decision, he suddenly lifted the net from his butterfly, releasing it from the mesh. Dazed, the insect stuttered from his lap and travelled the short distance to the grass, where it stayed, trembling. Toby stretched out his fingers, aiming to gently help the butterfly take off, but was startled by the distant sound of the front door slamming – thud! - followed by the familiar roar of his brother's motorbike erupting furiously into life. He drew back his fingers, distracted. What now?

Seconds later, Mum came through the patio doors and sat down with him on the steps. Putting her arm around his shoulders, she joined him in gazing at the still-shivering butterfly on the grass. Toby turned to face her. Sighed. "I shouldn't…" he murmured, then stopped.

Mum didn't reply at first but then smiled and pointed. "Look!" The butterfly was beginning to stretch her wings out, delicately and slowly.

Toby's face began to crease into a grin, only to halt mid-way. Alex?" he queried.

His Mum hugged him - tight. "It's alright; he has to spread his wings, but he'll always come back to us."

Toby thought about this for a while, then nodded. Accepting. They both watched as the butterfly finally rose into the air and fluttered away.

# 4
# RUTH

7.30 a.m. As she waits, the melody tiptoes through the dimpled clefts of her thoughts. Piano music; soft and hesitant, it brings no answers but only emphasises the multitude of questions: questions, she realises, will not now receive an adequate response. Coupled with the oppressively cloying atmosphere of the cell, these impressions are neither comforting nor threatening. Merely in attendance. Yet, if she permitted, the feelings could build and rise within her; could easily over-power her outward serenity, emitting like a tsunami gathering up frustrations as it travels across the oceans, finally releasing the tightly coiled force and vigour upon reaching land. If she allowed, she could discharge all the factors that have led to this very morning; that will today lead to her quick and seemingly facile demise. But she doesn't. She keeps them suppressed. Has to.

Externally, she portrays a very different character from the woman revealed at her last public appearance. Putting behind her the smart persona of just three weeks before - no longer needing to hide her soul from a curious but condemning audience - the well-cut black suit and white silk blouse is replaced with a simple grey dress. Freshly bleached and coiffured hair is abandoned in favour of a scraped back ponytail. She is stripped of false eyelashes, of thick make-up, of peroxide blonde. Only her demeanour is the same; calm and composed. Eyes without depth. Revealing nothing.

Forcing herself out of stupor, to focus on what needs to be done, she lowers her eyes to the letter she has been writing to her solicitor. Re-reads the opening:

*Dear Mr Simmons,*

*Just to let you know that I am still feeling alright.*

*The time is seven o'clock am - everyone is simply wonderful in Holloway. This is just for you to console my family with the thought that I did not change my way of thinking at the last moment.*

*Or break my promise to David's mother...*

She stops reading. Frowns. What she has written seems trite. Childish. Yet, what more is there to say? She *has* kept her promise and she is not going to go against this vow – not now, not ever. That is how it will be; an eye for an eye. She picks up the pen to write more – to add some poignant reflections perhaps - but then hesitates, imagining she can sense an unfamiliar presence. Someone besides the two silent women officers at the far side of the room. Is the man coming now? Is it time? She had thought it was supposed to happen at 9 a.m. But maybe there has been a change to the agenda – a change that no-one has told her about. She listens intently, her nerves and muscles strained and tense in concentration. Poised on the very brink of composure, close to tipping over. Waiting. No man appears, and the steady tick of the clock reassures her that she still has time... for the moment. She positions the pen on the paper and, with no further words of wisdom to impart, just concludes with what she needs to:

*... Well Mr Simmons, I have told the truth, and that's all I can do. Thanks once again,*

*Goodbye,*

*Ruth.*

She places this letter alongside the others she has written, with a faint air of fulfilment. Totality. The last missal completed, she has now concluded her business; crossed the t's and dotted the i's. Nothing more to do. A conclusion – admittedly insignificant – to her twenty-eight years.

Now released from her self-imposed duties, she drifts into daydreams. It seems strange to her how at this moment – of all times – she feels surrounded by a dense numbness. Effective and protective, it's as if mind has disengaged from body and is just hovering innocuously by the side. Impassive. Unemotional. An odd feeling. The body's way of coping with an unimaginable situation? Perhaps. Her gaze drops down tiredly and focuses on the hands resting patiently on her lap. Thin and frail. She reflects that they ought to appear more threatening, more menacing; should at least look capable for the worst of wrongdoing. However, they are just their palely inoffensive selves, merely seeming startled at where they've found themselves. She allows herself a wry smile at this fanciful thought.

8.15 a.m. Now other sounds join the ticking of the clock and the melodies of her mind. Noises from outside; the faint hum of a crowd drawing closer – shouting, jeering, cheering. Then something different. Something which seems out of place in its delicacy and elegance. Still sitting, she strains her neck towards the window in an attempt to decipher the more subtle resonance which is mingling with the harsh jeers of humanity. Cello music? Yes… She can't recall the name of the melody and doesn't search her mind too hard to do so; instead she lets the notes float over and around her – low and resonant, they provide an easy and undemanding accompaniment to her indistinct thoughts. She closes her eyes and yields to the music…

\*\*\*

8.30 a.m. She snaps her eyes open as now – finally - she hears the footsteps she has been waiting for. Thud… Thud… Portentous echoes in distant corridors. Slow. Rhythmical. Marking time; ticking closer to an inevitable conclusion; no possibility of altering their course or destiny. She sighs, feeling her heartbeat betray her by speeding up in fear; in direct contrast to her controlled resignation, it nudges her into reflecting on the fragility of her humankind. Then, unexpectedly, kindles a tiny grain of optimism, even in this, the direst of circumstances. Is it so wrong to hope for a last-minute reprieve?

Thud… Closer and louder. She holds up her hands now to observe whether they will tremble, but they remain unmoving. No betrayal of guilt or remorse. Is this normal? Surely they should shiver and shake at the very thought of what is to come? But then, *why* should they? They are only two pieces of apparatus, a means to an end; the real villain is not to be found on her surface but rather far within the very core of her fiercely-beating heart. The part of her that is only visible to the soul. That is where the little knot of jealousy and revenge has grown and festered over past months, finally – explosively – discharging into the deadly deed which has placed her where she is now.

Thud… Nearly here. The noise of the footsteps overwhelms the soft sound of the clock, eclipsing the reassurance of its tick. The measured paces are all that matter now. The steps pause. Wait. And, as the heavy oak door begins to open, she rises quickly from the table, spilling the chair backwards onto the floor in her haste. An open door. He stands there, unspeaking. In his hands a… belt? A strap? Disregarding this, she looks up to him; face to face. Her eyes cool and daring, his curious and wondering. Moments pass and then he lowers his eyes to the ground. Shakes his head in a tiny movement.

Finally, he clears his throat uneasily and prepares to speak. His voice – soft and low - doesn't correspond with his unforgiving, solidly-built frame and although his expression remains guarded, she still catches a fleeting glimpse of compassion in his deep brown eyes as he addresses her. "Ruth? It's time."

# 5

# THE GRAVE WHISPERER

I walk down the hill towards the mourners. Stopping a respectful distance away, I prop my spade against a nearby tree and wait. Watch the small group of people down by the open grave, huddling together against the penetrating breeze. A family unit. Elderly husband, adult children, teenage grandchildren, friends. Paying their respects.

I look up to the wintry sky and breathe deeply, reflecting, not for the first time, on the uniqueness of my profession. An unusual trade, of course - I know this has been said many a time; to my face and behind my back, no doubt. But there are definitely worse ways to make a living. This way – *my* way - does, at least, have significance. An importance. I think so, anyway. It's not an occupation for everyone, understandably, not for the squeamish or the sensitive; certainly not for those who would take it all too much to heart, dwelling incessantly on the meaning of life. Or death, obviously. To me, there's nothing morbid or strange about bringing closure to a life in the way a person wanted. Not at all. This job is in my blood; it's what my father did, and his father before him. No reason to do anything else: it's my vocation.

A few minutes pass and the mourners slowly shuffle out of their united cluster and wind-stagger back along the cobbled path. Focussed only on returning to the comparative warmth of the church. I remain still, waiting for any last-minute revisiting. Sometimes that happens - a relative or friend returning to the grave to express one last goodbye; unable, perhaps, to sever that final link. Not this time. So, retrieving my spade, I slowly make my way down the hill.

Without the bolstering relatives, the grave seems lonely. Vulnerable. I peer down and nod in approval at the extravagant coffin. Burnished oak. Brass fittings. Sparsely adorned with dry scatters of earth and a single red rose, it is placed perfectly symmetrically in the shallow plot. As it should be. A job well done. Nevertheless, there's no time for any more such observations and pleasantries now: it's time for me to do *my* job.

Placing the spade carefully beside me – pretences not necessary now - I hunker down and then extend my right arm until my fingertips make contact with the shining brown wood below. Cool and dry to touch. I wait. Not a career for an impatient man, this. In fact, sometimes I've had to remain graveside for a good few hours before being able to complete my duties. It doesn't make any difference; I don't mind. As is my custom, I use the time to reflect on my duties and missions from over the years. Right back from when I started, at the age of eighteen. It helps me to get into the zone. However, I have to admit, though, my assignments so far have been relatively ordinary: delivering a final bouquet of flowers to a loved one, reassuring another of the deceased's eternal love, sampling one last pint of favourite ale... Dull, to be quite honest. Not that it is the norm for our family to have had similarly boring experiences, of course. For example, my grandfather was continuously boasting about the time when he was asked to...

Ah - I have contact! Extraordinarily quick: probably the fastest I've ever had, to be truthful. As the familiar tingle runs through my fingers, my mind quivers and then gradually adjusts to the voice which is beginning to stake its claim. Sorry; *her* claim. And she is insistent. Resolute. A strong personality who is unwavering in her demands. I listen intently, suddenly becoming conscious of my morality and principles fighting the words at the exact same time as my thoughts are obediently succumbing to them. Confused – needing time to reflect - I snatch my hand away from the coffin, hoping for separation. An interval in which to consider. To think. No, the vibes are so strong that they continue to invade my emotions, my conscience, even without physical connection. I have no choice but to listen. Finally, my soul shudders violently. Surrenders.

*He slowly rises from crouched position. Picks up spade. Swiftly walks along cobbled path towards church. Towards mourners. Vigorously long strides. Reaches them in matter of moments. Ignores turned heads, startled expressions, monosyllabic exclamations. Moves towards grieving husband. Husband stares, brow furrowing. Slow motion. Spade raised to optimum height. Then, suddenly, exaggeratedly accelerated speed. Blow struck on forehead. Husband falls. Blood. Screams. One word from protagonist: "Adulterer."*

Directly after, my soul quickly agitates back, returning me to *me*. Staring at the chaotic scene around me, I open my mouth to give explanations – apologies? – but then realise I can't; not without yielding my whole identity and purpose. And I will not be the one to do that – to bring generations of our profession to a standstill. No. Silently, I shake my head: it is what it is. Finally, I heft the blood-stained spade back onto my shoulder and walk away.

Back up the hill, back into the myriad colours of the sunset.

# 6
# IDENTITY

In the classroom next to mine, Ms Speakly practised kick boxing every morning from 8.30 to 9.00. Well, I assume it was kick-boxing; certainly sounded like it, anyway. It was – it would seem - an essential start to her day. Less auspicious for me, my ears regularly throbbing with the persistent *thud-thud-thud* coming through the gossamer-thin wall. She did what she had to, I suppose. Though *why* she had to was a mystery to me.

Trouble was, I didn't feel I could even ask her what she was doing, let alone whether she would desist – I didn't know her well enough for that. She'd only started at our school that term, three weeks earlier - mornings only - and we hadn't yet advanced beyond, "Assembly first thing today," and "Heads up, the Head's observing on Wednesday." Certainly not enough of a connection for me to ask favours, so I put up with it. Nevertheless, she intrigued me.

Occasionally after school, with my mind drifting from my marking and ears blissfully free from thudding, I wondered what Ms Speakly did with her afternoons. She wasn't old enough to be a part-time, easing-down-to-retirement sort of teacher. Far from it: she had energy – lots of it. When it was her class's turn for Games, she was out there like an optimistic Olympian, displaying techniques, joining in, being a thoroughly good 'role model,' as the Head would say. So there must be another reason as to why she didn't teach full-time. A good reason, obviously. Perhaps she had family commitments. Or a second job, possibly something related to the kick-boxing regime. Maybe - when I knew her better - I would ask her.

A few weeks after term had started, on a Tuesday morning in February, I noticed a difference in the thudding sound from next door. It seemed more... *insistent* somehow. I paused in setting up my Literacy PowerPoint and waited. Yes, it *was* different; more a *thwack-thud-thwack-thud* than the previous *thud-thud-thud.* This intrigued me even more than before – this time I simply *had* to find out what was going on.

Tiptoeing out of my classroom, I eased myself against the dividing wall and surreptitiously peeped through the glass panel of the door. I didn't spot her immediately; she'd pulled down the blinds and hadn't yet turned on the lights. I couldn't make much out until my eyes acclimatised but I then spotted her tall figure executing some rather scary looking moves over in the book corner. She seemed to be chopping objects – I couldn't see exactly what - in half. Strange. But I barely had time to register this before she turned, her piercing eyes probing right towards me.

Quickly, I pulled back from the small window, my heart thumping frantically with the embarrassment of being caught snooping. Scuttling back to my classroom and closing the door behind me, I sank down heavily at my desk. What on earth had she been doing? And was there a connection with her afternoon activities? To be honest, I was now even more confused than previously.

The rest of the day passed in a colourless blur. I taught the children in some sense of normality – I must have done, for I'd have known about it from them if I hadn't. But whilst I was carrying out my duties like some sort of automated teaching machine, the images of Ms Speakly briskly chopping, chopping, chopping, were firmly at the forefront of my consciousness.

That night at home, I made a decision: I would follow Ms Speakly during her next afternoon off to find out exactly what her second job was; or at least to see what she got up to after her usual morning teaching.

So, the following lunchtime, feigning a migraine, I made my excuses to a none-too-pleased Head. Left school. Hunching down in my car until I spotted Ms Speakly come out of the building, I then drove a careful distance behind her as she headed towards town. A few miles in, she parked up behind a large office block and jumped out of her car, holding a large black bag. I pulled in a few metres away and followed, ducking behind the building's wall just in time to hear her speak loudly into the intercom: "Ms Bateman, technician."

As she was admitted, I bit my lip and frowned. *Bateman?* If technician was her second job, why use a different name? And in that case, which of her names was correct? If either?

I'd only been standing there for a few minutes, when I heard the click of the main door and Ms Speakly/Bateman exited the offices. Her mobile clamped to her ear, she uttered only two words as she swiftly returned to her car: "Job done."

I left it a while before returning to my own car – not wanting to be spotted – but when I eventually did so, I suddenly heard the sound of approaching sirens. As I sat in the car, I watched as an ambulance and police car pulled up to the same block of offices that Ms Speakly had just left. My ears flooded with a dull roar as a stretchered body was then carried out from the building. It was some time before I could trust myself to drive home.

That evening, the events of the afternoon flashed backwards and forwards in my mind as I tried to make sense of what I'd seen. Had the two events – Ms Speakly entering the building and some poor soul being injured/killed – been related? Or was it just a nasty coincidence? But then, why did Ms Speakly appear to have two surnames? Surely that was suspicious in itself? Only people of a dubious nature, or those with something to hide would have a double identity. Like a spy, for example, or even... well, perhaps, in fact, an...

"Assassin!" I finished confidently the next morning, after giving the Head all the details. After much deliberation, I'd figured it was what needed to be done.

He blinked, momentarily speechless.

"It would explain everything," I reasoned. "She obviously teaches in the mornings – no better cover-up than that, after all – and in the afternoons, she's a hit m – woman." I stopped, relieved. I'd done it: told him.

The Head cleared his throat. "Mr Johnson," he began, having finally found his voice. "You realise how crazy this... *accusation* sounds?"

I nodded. "Well, I realise it's unusual – I hardly believed it myself at first, but -"

He cut me off. "Quite. You also realise that any teacher we take on, here at Merlywild Junior, is thoroughly vetted before they start – as you yourself were, obviously."

"Y-yes, but..." I wasn't sure how to proceed now – I thought at least the Head would have volunteered to look into my theory, even if he had initially been sceptical.

"Furthermore..." he pursed his lips; I'd seen that

37

expression before, it was the 'I will not tolerate fools in my school' look. "*Furthermore*, I am not at all happy about you faking illness so that you can go on a wild goose chase to spy on one of my staff; a member of staff who has, you'll be interested to hear, the very best references and credentials. *The best.*" He paused, then peered at me over top of his glasses. "I can only think that you have fabricated this story out of some sort of jealousy; perhaps you think that you have competition for future promotions from Ms Speakly?"

I opened my mouth and then closed it again. There was obviously no use in continuing this conversation; the best I could do now was to get out before I put my foot in it even further…

*** 

Trudging down the corridor towards my classroom, doubts began to trickle in about my previously watertight theory. The Head *was* right in that Ms Speakly would have had police checks and all sorts before joining our school – perhaps there were perfectly good reasons for her actions; *perhaps* I was, in fact, just being overly imaginative? Sensationalist, even?

"Mr Johnson – a word please?" Ms Speakly's strident tones interrupted my thoughts before I reached my door. She didn't wait for me to answer, but waded straight in. "Just to let you know that my afternoon job is that of a peripatetic computer consultant. That's all." She stared at me as if daring me to refute this.

"Ah… Um…" I petered out, stammeringly and blushingly embarrassed.

Ms Speakly laughed. It was a strange, non-humorous sound. "I suppose it's a mistake anyone could make," she said. "Well, someone who has too much time on their hands, possibly? Anyway, no hard feelings, I suppose."

"Thanks." I turned to go – relieved – but then something occurred to me. I swivelled back round again. "But, how did you know I'd...?"

She didn't let me finish. Now her voice was harder, a hint of steeliness running through it. It chilled my blood as she replied. "I think we'll just leave it there, shall we? Draw the line."

# 7

# OUTBURST OF THE SOUL

Murmuring. Then exclaiming. Lex waits several minutes for the excited group of students to disseminate before finally moving over to the notice board himself. Hoping desperately that his hunch is correct, he reads the poster carefully. He's right; it *is* the formal announcement of the Rachmaninoff Piano Concerto Competition: to be held on the 21st April at 2 p.m. Just over six months' time. He takes a deep breath. Right. Here it is. The chance to have his name engraved in gold on that esteemed and coveted honours board. To change his status from merely being Lex, undergraduate music student, to Alex Jameson, Rachmaninoff Prize Winner. Kudos.

Time for action. Walking purposefully back to his lodgings just a few roads away, he retrieves his Rachmaninoff manuscripts. All four concertos. Which to choose? Laying his copies on the small table that serves as his desk, he flicks them open, one by one. Softly hums the first few notes of every first page in turn.

He immediately rejects the F# minor; too naive, not... *showy* enough to impress. What about the C minor; the most popular? Is it *too* well known, though – *too* fashionable perhaps? Would the judges be measuring his every note against the so-perfect recordings of Barenboim, Sarah Chang, or even Rachmaninoff himself? Quite possibly.

So... No.3. D minor. He bites his lip as he reflects on

this piece: one of the most demanding concertos in the piano repertoire, it would be a superb chance to show off an astounding technique, particularly in the ferocious climax. Also, unlike most musicians, he would opt to play the chordal original, rather than the lighter, toccata-like version. Really make an impact on the judges… Yet… He frowns and returns to the C minor once more, staring at the effusive opening chords until his eyes blur over into a miasma of black and white swirls. Considers. He has been drawn to this piece ever since first hearing it as a child; perhaps it would be best to play it – the concerto he's truly at one with; the music that really *means* something to him? Go with his gut instinct. Yes. He nods to himself as he carefully tucks the C minor manuscript into his rucksack and marches back towards the Music College, intent on securing one of the acoustically-better practice rooms.

***

Weeks pass. Practise. Slide into months. Practise. More practise. Mornings, afternoons, evenings. Practise. Devoured by the music, Lex develops a haunted expression on his already gaunt face. He discourages, then completely discontinues, interaction with his fellow students; anything apart from his practise is obviously a waste of time. Of energy, too. He lives to practise piano. He practises to live piano. Soon, his eyes smoulder into burning crotchets of distraction. Cheeks hollow. But he continues to practise. And practise. Even at night, when sleep should free him from his exertions, he still has no respite from the haunting melodies; his fingers twitch nervily over quavers and semi-quavers, prohibiting the luxury of dream-free unconsciousness. His dogged aspirations overwhelm his body's need for rest; come the mornings he ignores his heavy eyes and cloudy thoughts and determinedly makes his way back to the piano. Continues to practise. And practise.

Eventually, the advent of 21st April penetrates the patchwork of months that have been interwoven and immersed with crotchets and quavers, semi-breves and minims. At 1.30.pm precisely, Lex joins five other competitors waiting outside the Amaryllis Fleming Hall. Sits down to wait. With his arms and legs crossed in a barrier against the risk of failure-contamination from his rivals, he mentally vows to let nothing threaten his self-belief. His very demeanour casts a powerful gloom over the small assembly until, eventually, every last resonance of chatter amongst the students fades away. Thus, with neither eye contact nor verbal exchange, the six pianists sit in bent-head silence until the doors are opened and the first name is called: Lex's.

Lex walks steadily down the aisle, past the audience, not acknowledging them, not *seeing* them. Slowly climbs the stairs to the stage. As he nears the piano, the single spotlight above flickers over the slight figure and then stabilises itself in directing the beam onto the black and white keys. Lex sits down at the antique Steinway grand and spends several moments adjusting the leather-bound stool. When satisfied, he looks over to the conductor and nods – a transitory but decisive movement. Places his hands on the piano keys, quietly exhaling as his fingertips meet the cool, smooth touch of ivory.

*Moderato: C minor.* Opening chords: sentinel, heavy, bell-like. As soon as he strokes these initial notes, he is immediately immersed in C minor. *Only* C minor, to the exclusion of all others. He is protected within the melody, even when it disperses and scatters into a rapid oscillating series of arpeggios, flowing into quick-fire semi-quavers.

Changes position; now he's merely a setting for the ever-responsive orchestra to discharge a dominant C, then D and back again to C. Imprinted aurally into his brain. Harmonies that both defend and shelter until – after an amount of melodic deliberation - they slide into E flat major; a brief cease-fire transition enabling a welcome reflection. Restoration.

Yet the relief is short-lived. Agitated and unstable developments now dip in and out of prominence; without guilt, they steal motives from several themes, gradually moulding into a new, enthralling concept. Then build into a gradual climax, suggesting that the first bars will be repeated – taunting – but finally presenting the theme as unique to the original statement. Such is her capriciousness. However, even *she* has to diminish and cease in due course. Finally, she does.

*Adagio sostenuto – Più animato – Tempo I: C♯ minor → E major.* Lex closes his eyes as he drifts into this movement, finally rediscovering and relishing the major key like a heat-starved Eskimo unexpectedly finding himself in the sunlight. Forgotten are angst-ridden E flats and severe C minor chords - now he can lose himself in simple arpeggiated major figures, accompanied by subtle-voiced flutes and clarinets who respect and follow his every notion. Having given all in their finest capability, his instrument-companions now lose interest and drift away, leaving Lex playing alone, disorientated in wistfulness and abstraction. Nevertheless, he then, with no prior notice or salutation, rallies with a final triumphant C D C, in a teasing imitation of the previous whimsical theme, bringing the movement to a nourishing and victorious finish.

*Allegro scherzando: E major → C minor → C major.* A

pause while Lex makes the emotional and spiritual changeover in mood and movement. Then the tiniest of nods to the strings enables them to begin their conversation; cellos to violins to cellos – back and forth. Lex breathes in the notes while he stretches his fingers, ready to interrupt the dialogue. Cymbals heralding his reply, which, when it commences, silences the whole orchestra with the agitated first theme. After the original fast tempo and musical drama ends, a lyrical premise is introduced by the oboe and violas. Then, following a long period of development while the tension is constructed and fostered, this theme maintains the motif already stated in the first movement. It's now time; time for Lex to guide the build-up, to lead the way to exquisite climax.

He raises his fingers briefly – waits - and in that split-second moment is hazily aware of some sort of low-level disturbance in the audience. Voices. Unrest. With a trace of annoyance and a defiant lack of curiosity, he quickly replaces his hands on the piano keys, intent on returning at once to the world which will sequester him. The one in which only he and the music exist. Satisfying. Insular. And so… unseeing of the exodus, unhearing of the warnings, he is fully immersed in his music. Captured. Even the well-meaning outsiders that urgently nudge Lex's shoulder are unfelt; ignored with no more concern than if they'd been the tiptoe of a butterfly on a blossoming buddleia. Unmindful.

He begins to affirm the heartfelt chords, bidding the orchestra of his mind fill in for the lack of physical instrumentalists. It seems fitting that he is now alone in the concerto, for the music will be his and his alone. Just himself at the piano, striving to be all to the music, just as the music is all to him. He can do it. There is no doubt.

He leans towards the concluding notes, anticipating and welcoming the C major that will bring the concerto to its rightful ending. When he plays the penultimate triad, a smile flickers across his face in readiness for closure... he reaches out for those notes which will make sense of the whole piece: the final chord. But, as he stretches to make contact, suddenly a colossal explosion freezes the moment – *his* moment – in mid-melody... Everything Lex has set out to do is eclipsed by this vicious and intrusive stranger. His music is sent into a cosmos of discord and dissension, never to be righted with that last and final chord. In a shattering of milliseconds, all diminishes into darkness and silence...

*'Yesterday, mid-way between the Royal College of Music and the Albert Hall, a gas explosion razed these two prestigious buildings down to their very foundations. There had been prior warnings of leaking gas which enabled officials to evacuate the area; however, there are reports of one casualty; a young man who refused to leave the concert hall whilst competing in a well-regarded competition. Despite valiant efforts to induce him to leave, he remained at the piano, continuing to perform. This student's name has not yet been released but he has already been compared to the stalwart musicians on the ill-fated Titanic, who continued making music even as the ship itself was sinking.*

*It was later disclosed that this young man will now receive the Rachmaninoff Piano Concerto Award he so coveted – posthumously...'*

*(Extract from the South Kensington Daily Times)*

# 8
# ABSORPTION

The first option. Squinting against the intense sunlight, I can just about make out greenly-silhouetted fronds suspended on palms punctuated by hairy coconuts. Beyond these, a whoosh of froth-edged waves provides a rhythmic accompaniment: back and forth, back and forth. I take a tentative step onto the white sand, my open-sandalled toes first gaining the grains and then almost immediately expelling them back again with a pleasing *squidge*. So… have I found it – is *this* it?

Still not entirely certain, I turn my head to the unexpected sound of children's' voices in the distance. Sea-away, I peer over to the dunes and coagulated undergrowth beyond. Spot a flurry of pre-teens, running, chasing, screaming through the foliage, down towards the beach. As they grow closer, I identify the set-up - a gang of about twelve lads chasing one smaller, blond-haired boy. Even from this distance, I can sense the fear in his eyes. Then, just sweat-smelling metres away, I am able to decode the gang's shrill chant as it resounds across the slight breeze. An intonation which scratches then etches uncomfortably into my senses: "Kill the beast – kill him now!"

*Ralph screamed, a scream of fright and anger and desperation. His legs straightened, the screams became continuous and foaming. He shot forward, burst the thicket, was in the open, screaming, snarling, bloody. He swung the stake and the savage tumbled over; but there were others coming toward him, crying out. He swerved as a spear flew past and then was silent, running.*

What is this – some sort of boyish game being played? No, it seems more than just that; the whole scenario is too intense – too powerful. It feels as if the gang are really out to kill this young boy; to extract his blood. Like animals. Should I try to intervene: is there anything I could do to stop them? But even as the thought flickers through my mind, I know that nothing can be done – these boys have to play out their predestination. It is the only way.

Nevertheless, I shudder. This is definitely not the right place; *not* the sanctuary I'm looking for.

As soon as my decision is made, the figures and landscape quickly blur into obscurity. Now rootless, I reconsider my method. My approach. Maybe this next time I should start right at the beginning and not just seize a random moment. So I do.

A chilly, windy day, this time in a city – a more austere, forbidding setting. Grey buildings. Grim expressions. Wartime? Well, no, I don't think so; just a dismal, black and white city representation. Interesting. I move closer, curious to find out more and, as I do so, I hear a clock striking. One… two… three… Unable to resist - through force of habit originating back to when I was very small - I count along with them. Nine… ten… eleven… twelve… thirteen… *Thirteen?* Have I found myself in some sort of dystopia – a kind of No-man's land?

I stare around, searching for clues – for any indications of my whereabouts. Just then, a tall man of about forty strides towards me, brushes past and enters through glass doors into the large building nearby. *Victory Mansions.*

After only a moment of hesitation, my curiosity wins out and I follow him in, a small cloud of gritty dust trailing behind the two of us. As the man makes for the stairs, I stand still, taking stock of my surroundings, noticing that the hallway smells unpleasantly of boiled cabbage and old rag mats. However, this observation seems unimportant as soon as I spot the huge coloured poster tacked to the far wall. It captures my attention straight away, initially because it's the only splash of colour in an otherwise bleached-dull hallway. Building. City, even. A depiction of an enormous face, probably more than a metre wide: a middle-aged man with a heavy black moustache and strikingly piercing eyes – the sort of eyes that seem to follow you about as you move. Below the picture runs the caption: BIG BROTHER IS WATCHING YOU. I nod in comprehension. Now I recognise where I am; I understand the regime under which the citizens here have to live. A regime of restrictions. Telescreens. Newspeak. Big Brother. Being watched and listened to. *You had to live – did live, from habit that became instinct – in the assumption that every sound you made was overheard, and, except in darkness, every movement scrutinised.* Is this how I want to relax; how I want to spend my time? I laugh out loud; the sound unnaturally bright in the grim and dull atmosphere of my surroundings. Not in a lifetime – this is far from being my haven…

Quickly, I stir myself to move on. This time, a large, pleasant meadow with shady trees leaning benignly over a pond of clear water. A thick, green hedge: on one side a ploughed field, on the other a gate leading to a small cottage by the roadside. When I see the grove of fir trees and the running brook, I assume this idyllic scene is complete. That is, until I notice the midnight-dark, white-starred foal tripping curiously towards me. *Now* the setting is perfect. I smile. Say his name quietly, to avoid startling him: *Black Beauty*.

*The first place that I can well remember was a large pleasant meadow with a pond of clear water in it. Some shady trees leaned over it, and rushes and water-lilies grew at the deep end. Over the hedge on one side we looked into a plowed field, and on the other we looked over a gate at our master's house, which stood by the roadside; at the top of the meadow was a grove of fir trees, and at the bottom a running brook overhung by a steep bank.*

Black Beauty snuffles my hand to see if I have food, and his velvety nose tickles my palm. I smile and stroke his face; trace the outline of the star on his head with one finger, slowly and gently. Perhaps I could be happy here – maybe this could be *my* place? Who wouldn't want to bask in lush meadows with the sun above and the rolling countryside beside? This is somewhere I could relax, could unwind, surely? However, I suddenly notice an elderly man coming from the house, halter and lead in hand.

Ignoring me, he places a weathered hand on the young foal's back. "Time to go, Beauty," he says. "Come; I'll get you ready for your new home." He leads the horse back across the meadow towards the house. Now my new companion is leaving, the greens and blues around me begin to disperse, slowly and unwaveringly fading into ambiguity.

I sigh at the closing of another chapter, another potential sanctuary gone. I know I mustn't despair, though; I still have time, can still find my haven. I just need to keep looking – to try perhaps just once more…

Now it's night-time. A distant owl hoots a lonely

accompaniment to the twinkling stars above. I'm standing in a street with old-fashioned lamp posts – Victorian? – cobbled roads and pavements. All the houses are in darkness, bar one. This particular home boasts a warm night-light glow at its uncurtained upstairs window. I involuntarily give a small gasp as I watch, for fluttering around against the light are four small figures. Flying!

*It was just at this moment that Mr. and Mrs. Darling hurried with Nana out of 27. They ran into the middle of the street to look up at the nursery window; and, yes, it was still shut, but the room was ablaze with light, and most heart-gripping sight of all, they could see in shadow on the curtain three little figures in night attire circling round and round, not on the floor but in the air.*

I nod in satisfaction, knowing exactly where I am. Exactly *who* is showcasing in this scenario. This is perfect. Nothing will change here – Peter will remain ever-young, refusing to submit to the angst of teen and adult life, causing mischief wherever he travels. Both spontaneous and predictable in his behaviour. Fun to be with – his very demeanour a sanctuary from the stresses and strains of reality. He will be an escape from worries, from parents, from school. I've made my choice. Confidently, I pick up the copy of 'Peter Pan' and take it over to the woman at the main counter. "I'd like this one, please."

She smiles – she seems to understand – and swipes my card with her zapper. "There you are, dear – I hope you enjoy it."

# 9
# THE BEST KIND OF VOYEURISM

It was the second week of Vera's exclusively in-home existence. Seven days after she'd finally returned from hospital, pronounced sharp of mind but unsteady of legs. Housebound, with carers – mostly youngsters in their early teens it seemed – bustling in morning and evening to assist with 'the essentials', Vera was now an inside person. Officially.

So yes, it had definitely been week two when the family had moved in next door. She'd been curious to know who was replacing old Mr Bennett now that he'd apparently been despatched to a local nursing home (grumpily and under duress, of that she was certain). She certainly wouldn't miss that sharp cane knocking on the wall when he thought her TV was on too loudly. Boorish brute! She never turned the volume beyond 19 - after all, she wasn't deaf; her hearing and eyesight were both excellent for a woman of 80. So the doctors had stated. No, the man was just a cantankerous old grouch. Nothing more, nothing less.

A cold Tuesday. Growling engines and slamming doors alerted her to an arrival of some kind; she had time, with the help of her frame, to position herself by her chair beside the window. Ready to observe. She surreptitiously adjusted the off-white nets for an optimum outlook – *curtain-twitching,* Albert would have pronounced, if he'd been alive and observing her. But then, she corrected herself, Albert taking notice of his wife wouldn't have been that probable; he'd more likely have been ensconced behind The Telegraph, moaning about The Results (what The Results might have been – she'd never thought to enquire). She supposed it didn't really matter now.

A car arrived soon after the large removal lorries - a family sedan which discharged several earphone-eared youths, unbending themselves from the confined space and blinking mole-like in the daylight. Vera raised an eyebrow. *Teenagers.* Soon after, a man and woman emerged, seemingly trying to urge their offspring into animation – *come on, help with all the boxes*. Eventually, the youths complied, slouching and grouching in the teenagerish way specially reserved for their generation.

When the family finally got themselves and their belongings inside the house, Vera sat back comfortably and listened to the goings-on; kettles being boiled, footsteps stomping upstairs to claim bedrooms, bursts of music and then the sternness of news on TV. She smiled to herself. She supposed that, after all, Mr Bennett had been correct in being able to hear her TV; the dividing walls between the two houses were obviously flimsier than she had realised. Of course, that meant that he himself had lived almost soundlessly - she'd rarely heard any noise from him, apart from the unrelenting tap-tap-tap of the complaining cane. In contrast, having this family next door was like listening to a serial on TV. A boisterous serial at that. But Vera didn't mind. In fact, she rather enjoyed it – certainly made a pleasant change from the radio.

Over the next few weeks, she tuned in more and more – perfectly harmlessly, she justified - to the trials and tribulations of life next door. She celebrated when the older teenager – Archie - got his mock GCSE results; several more Bs and As than he, or his parents, had been expecting. She worried when Steve the cat trod on a piece of glass and was ferried to the vet, his bushy tail sticking out indignantly from the plastic animal carrier as they all hurried down the path. She sympathised when rows about messy bedrooms and lost homework had pierced her ears; she'd never had children of her own – Albert had never fancied the idea – but she could empathise as well as the next woman. More so, perhaps.

Many of these offspring-induced incidences caused Vera to ponder what her life would've been like if she and Albert *had* produced children. Each time the thought occurred, she shook her white head, with no definite conclusion attained. Things would have been very different, she supposed. Enhanced? Possibly. Instead of being sitting indoors in her chair, some kindly but tired, middle-aged daughter might have been pushing her around in a wheelchair to the shops, urging her to purchase padded foot warmers and bulky incontinence pads. Hmmm. Vera shrugged a little. Maybe not, then. It wasn't as if she was unhappy with her life, after all. No, she was perfectly content with her little world, even restricted as it was now to her own four walls. Especially now she had company next door. Undemanding and insulating company.

As the weeks passed, the family took up most of Vera's waking thoughts. She began to identify the pattern of their days; most seemed to follow a fairly unchanging routine with the wife leaving the house first – Katie was a librarian apparently – followed by the teenagers, separately, never together. Vera often worried that one or all of them would be late; surely 8.45 was cutting it too short when school normally started at 9? It wasn't as if they hurried once they had departed either - she could often still see them lingering in the cul-de-sac a good ten minutes after the front door had slammed. The husband? Well, to her annoyance, Vera hadn't yet been able to find out what Andrew did for a living; the assumption was that he mostly worked at home, for he kept odd hours with no regularity to them. Or perhaps he did shift work? She wasn't sure. Either way, weekdays were reasonably quiet until around four in the afternoon, when the family members started to arrive home, one by one. Then the house became animated, with the different interactions and exchanges resounding through the dividing walls, the tone depending on what kind of a day each person had experienced.

Naturally, it was weekends that Vera enjoyed the most; the two days when the family were constantly in and out, friends were invited, parties were held. Much more going on. More arguments too; she supposed it was because they were all contained in a relatively small space. Such were the ups and downs of family life, she surmised, in the gaps whilst waiting for the next instalment to begin.

However, things had changed recently. The atmosphere next door was different somehow. Soured. Vera couldn't pinpoint exactly when it had happened; it had been a gradual adjustment, over several days. There hadn't been, she thought, the usual frenetic bursts of life and animation ringing out. No; now there were long silences. Hushed voices. One-sided phone calls, terse with 'Yes' and 'Ok', and 'I see'. Several times, Vera shuffled her frame right over to the wall and pressed her ear against the flowery wallpaper to hear better, but was none the wiser. Even the teenagers had stopped playing their music so loudly. It was like someone had died. Well no – not exactly that – but what, she couldn't tell.

She didn't like this new ambience, this atmosphere unpunctuated by the bursts of music or snatches of laughter that she was used to hearing. It was almost as if the family were now too afraid to shout, to chatter, to make noise - were trying not to tempt fate by doing so. But why? How? Was it because of Vera herself; were they now aware that she could hear every word, every sound, causing them to tip-toe around, afraid to disclose anymore of themselves than they already had? Vera blushed at this thought. Surely she couldn't be blamed for just *being there?* Listening, albeit inadvertently. Was she expected to wear furry earmuffs to block their voices out or something? She chuckled to herself at the very thought. No, that would be totally unreasonable: it couldn't be.

Drugs then, perhaps. Maybe Archie, or even Sophie or Jason had ventured into the dark world of narcotics – possibly that crack cocaine stuff she'd heard about on the news - and were fighting a terrible battle against addiction? A battle which was affecting the whole family in their endeavour to get their child – or *children*, perish the thought – back on the straight and narrow. But then… wouldn't there be arguments, if this were the case? Pleading? Shouting? Crying? No, it was the relative silence which was the perturbing thing about the change in mood next door; if drugs had been the problem there would have been a great deal more commotion, she was sure of it.

It could, of course, be money worries. There was a possibility that in buying the house, the family had stretched themselves just a little too far. Vera nodded sagely to herself. Especially with Andrew not seeming to be working that much; it couldn't be easy feeding and clothing three large teenagers on one steady wage, let alone paying what was probably a hefty mortgage payment each month too. Hmm. It didn't explain the silences though, for surely you had to talk about these things, figure out solutions for getting through them. Unlike Albert though, she thought wryly; he had been the type who didn't invite her opinion at all - just told her what was what, usually well after the event. She had accepted this at the time; it was as it was. But modern couples, well, they were different, weren't they? They discussed their problems. Even if it made for an argument, it was how things were done nowadays.

So that would rule out divorce then, for there would have to be a great many disagreements before that happened, not just a gradual cooling, surely? Even though couples tended to go for separations much more easily than in her day. Not necessarily a bad thing, of course, although the TV would have you think otherwise. That Jeremy Kyle show, in particular - one of those shows that you couldn't help yourself watching, despite the sheer trashiness of it all. However, Vera did concede that if a relationship wasn't working, then a harmonious split was the obvious solution. Now it was socially acceptable. Indeed, if this had been the case forty years ago, well, who knows how things would have turned out for herself and Albert...

She sighed. All this thinking wasn't helping the situation next door, and she still wasn't sure what to do about it. It had been several days now, almost a week. She couldn't concentrate on anything else; abandoning any pretence of TV watching or radio listening, she sat, hour after hour, focussing solely on the problem of what was wrong with the family. What she could do to help.

Finally she realised, on the eighth day, that there was only one thing she *could* do, and that was to visit them, difficult though this would be with her legs being as they were. However, there was nothing else she could think of, despite all the different assistances which had occurred to her (calling the police or the social services, or asking her carer to intervene). No, she needed to sort this out by herself, and in person too.

It was ten o'clock on a Wednesday morning and all three teenagers were still at home. Odd in itself for they clearly should've been at school. Stranger still, the husband and wife had gone out together, an hour or so earlier. Perhaps she could talk to the teenagers then... Maybe if she chatted to them, they could offer some insight into what had happened. Not that she'd ask them outright, obviously, but they might just give something away. It was possible.

Decision made, Vera was just slowly rising from her armchair, determined on her mission, when she heard a loud thud – next door's front door banging closed. She paused, mid-stand, as the wife's voice called out, "We're back!"

Running footsteps and then a teenager – Archie? – "How did it go, what did they say?"

Now the husband, "She got the all clear – everything's fine; there's nothing to worry about."

Huge whoops of delight resounded through Vera's small living room, followed quickly by clatters of... crockery? Glasses? Obviously time for a cup of tea or something stronger. Celebrating.

Phew... Vera sank back heavily in her chair. *A medical*

*predicament. All sorted out.* She closed her eyes and exhaled deeply, allowing the strong feeling of joy to flood over her. Things would be fine now. Back to normal.

# 10
# A WOMAN SCORNED

"Why your Granddad's shed?" Chloe asked doubtfully.

Jo smiled. "It's got exactly the right atmosphere, don't you think?"

"S'pose." Chloe shivered. Indicated towards the large cauldron in the centre of the room. "Shall we, then?"

Nodding, Jo opened up her bag and took out a book: Spells for the Betrayed.

This time it was Becky who had reservations. "Seriously? You actually believe this is going to work?"

Jo's eyes narrowed. "Well, if it doesn't at midnight, then it never will." She reached back into the bag, now bringing out a length of twine.

Becky sighed. "Jo, even if you succeed in breaking them up, he chose her over you – would you really want him back?"

Jo snorted. "Course not! No, I want… revenge. On him and her, whoever she is."

"You don't know?" Chloe was surprised.

Jo shook her head. "Not yet. But it doesn't matter, the spell will still find her."

"You don't really believe you can curse them?" Becky sighed. "Look – why don't you scratch Matt's car or something instead? Not this - this is just… weird!"

Exasperated, Jo looked up from her bag-rummaging. "Well, weird or not, you promised you'd help. Now, make yourself useful and add rainwater to the cauldron." She handed over a container.

Eyebrows raised, Becky nevertheless removed the lid and tipped the water in.

Jo nodded. "Now, Chloe – if you could light this and place it over there…"

Chloe took out her lighter and lit the slim, tapered candle, taking a step back from the pungent aroma that resulted. "God, that stinks!"

"It's very potent. And expensive. Still, it'll be worth it…" Jo chuckled disconcertingly.

Before the other two could comment, they were distracted by the cauldron hissing and spitting out dirty-blue smoke.

"Ah, it's ready," Jo declared, picking up the candle and motioning for them to gather around. When she spoke again, her voice was low. Mesmerising:

"The two who have wronged me must suffer as I've suffered As I will, so mote it be."

On her last word, she quickly held the twine over the candle. As soon as the flame had burnt the rope in two, she ran out with the pieces into the darkness of the deserted allotment, and buried them shallowly in the earth. Chloe and Becky hovered in the shed doorway, unsure what they were supposed to do. However, Jo soon returned.

"Right," she said, in normal tones. "We just need to wait for the candle to completely burn, then the spell will be cast."

Becky glanced at the fetidly flickering flame. "That'll take ages."

"Whatever." Jo shrugged, sitting down on a packing crate and folding her arms.

\*\*\*

Eventually, when dusk slid into evening, the solitary candle sputtered for a few seconds and then extinguished. Total blackout.

Hands shaking slightly, Chloe managed to flick on her lighter and hold it up.

Jo smirked. "It worked." she hissed triumphantly, "It worked!"

Puzzled, Chloe turned to Becky. Gasped. Her friend's face was totally obscured by yellow-pus-seeping boils and pustules.

Chloe swung back to Jo. "Did you know?"

Jo exhaled noisily. "Let's just say I had my suspicions."

# 11
# PERFORATIONS

"I've never wanted kids - you know that!" Jo frowned. Why was Paul being so stupid? She slammed her hands onto her hips and an angry crimson began spreading across her neck. "Well? Did you think that I'd change my mind; is that what you were relying on?"

Her husband sighed. His tongue felt as if coherent conversation was a dim and distant novelty from times past. "No - well, maybe... oh, I don't know! People *do* change, their *views* change; I thought perhaps..."

"Bloody hell, Paul – I thought you knew me better than that!" Jo shook her head and stared at him incredulously. Was this really the man she'd known and loved for over seven years? Did he really believe that her beliefs would alter so radically, just because *his* had? She took a deep breath and forced her voice to sound calm. "Look, we've had this conversation – both before and after we got married, just to make sure; we *agreed*..."

"But I didn't know how I'd feel five years along the line, did I – how could I?" Paul was finally spurred into anger. "Yes, I love our life as it is, but kids would enhance it; make it even better. When I see Martin with his two, well, it's what I want now. It's the future. It's permanent."

"What we have isn't permanent?" Jo was genuinely mystified. She shook her head again in an attempt to clear the miasma of confusion. How could Paul have been going through this quandary without her even realising?

Then she frowned again – trust his bloody brother to be involved somehow. Yes, she knew Paul adored his niece and nephew – who wouldn't love those two cuties? – but to let them sway him to the extent that he had misgivings about whether his own marriage was enough for him… She exhaled deeply, disbelieving and on the verge of tears.

Spotting the tell-tale glint in her eyes, Paul put his arm around her, urging her down onto their large sofa. He stroked her hand for a moment before speaking again. "Love, I know this must be a shock. I should've said something before now, but I thought – *hoped* – you might come round to the same way of thinking."

Jo snorted loudly. Shoving Paul's hand back on his lap, causing him to wince, she sat up straight. Turned to him. "Look. We have a bloody good life, surely you can see that? We do what we want, when we want. No encumbrances." She paused; now the words were out in the open, they sounded a little cold. Selfish, even. She tried again. "Once you bring another… *aspect* into the equation, everything changes. Come on Paul, we've both seen it, haven't we? Dave and Carol… Tim and Becky… Couples that seemed to be perfect, invincible even – they've fallen out over the smallest things, become bitter, grown apart…" She paused, allowing the words to hover in the air like tiny, stinging gnats.

However, Paul didn't falter. "So you think our marriage can't survive a couple of ankle-biting challenges, is that it? He shook his head mock-sorrowfully. "Poor state of affairs then."

"No! You know it's not like that – we're strong, we've had to be." The memories of joint parental opposition at their mixed-race relationship still niggling, Jo tried harder to get her point across. "We've come through a lot, you and I – different backgrounds, upbringings, careers – but," and here she waggled a finger in Paul's face, "corny as it sounds, our love keeps us together."

Paul seemed confused. "Well yeah, I never said it doesn't. If anything, I want to *add* to the love – that can't be wrong, can it?"

"No – not for couples who share that sentiment – of course not. We've always been adamant that the two of us are enough, though... Well, we *have* been; now it's obviously changed. *You've* changed. And, well, I don't know if we can get through this..." Jo's voice trailed away.

Paul spoke softly. "All I want you to do is to think about it – *rethink* your viewpoint. For me, please, Josie. After all, if I can change my mind, then maybe you can too."

Jo shrugged. "I will think about it, yes, you deserve that much. But I can tell you now, categorically, that I won't alter my stance on this. Ever."

"Mmm..." Paul resumed stroking his wife's hand gently. "What if your mind was changed for you?"

Unexpectedly, Jo grinned. "Sorry, but that's the beauty of contraception – 99.9 per cent protection, you know. And accidents are reserved for teenage girls and menopausally-careless middle-agers." Ha – she had him there!

Paul changed tactics. "When you're holding your baby in your arms... a mixture of you and me; my hair and your features or –"

"-Yeah, whatever, it's not going to happen." Jo was growing impatient now; there was a documentary starting soon and she really wanted to watch it. Preferably without a whining husband in the periphery.

"I mean... suppose our contraception did let us down...?" Paul's voice was gruff.

Jo shuddered, then sighed loudly. "I really don't know, seeing as how we're both so against abortion. I take it you haven't changed your mind about that, too?"

Paul paled, shaking his head vigorously. "Definitely not!"

"Well, we've been okay so far – no false alarms or scares – so I reckon we can pretty much rely on the condoms we use. Yes? Hon, this feels like we're just travelling around in circles... Let's leave it – I'm too knackered to argue." Reaching for the remote, Jo pressed 'on' and stared thankfully at the screen, wondering blearily why she'd been so exhausted this past week or so...

Paul opened his mouth to protest and then, sensing futility, shook his head. Rising, he stumbled into the kitchen and plonked himself onto a chair. Stared down at the pale-blond floor; patterns of tiny flecks of colour... Spots, marks, dots... Pinpricks... As his eyes blurred, these images merged into recollections from several weeks ago: himself with a needle, carefully perforating every last one of the condoms in the box on the bedside table...

# 12
# A PERFECT DAY

Sophie opens her eyes slowly, little by little. Listening for the call of birdsong that will alert her to the time, she is gratified when the sudden crescendo of chirruping and rustling signifies 6.30. She yawns, blinks at the thin shaft of sunlight peeping through the curtains, and lifts her head a fraction towards the window. A sunny summer day. Time to put aside worries and anxieties; time to celebrate the here and now. Life. Determined, she reaches for her inner strength and - not wanting to relinquish the gossamer-thin thread - hugs it to her, commissioning it to satiate her mind and soul. Fulfil.

Now closing her eyes again, she smiles in pleasure as the delicate piano chords begin to tiptoe through her consciousness, like droplets of dew befitting the early morning haze. She recognises the soft and steady drum beat, closely followed by the opening melody. Poignant and pure.

\*\*\*

Flip-flops in hand, I walk barefoot across the damp grass, grinning as I spot him strolling towards me. We share a kiss – brief and sweet – and then he takes my shoes in his hand. My arm in the other. "Come on, Soph; I've found the perfect spot! Close your eyes now – no peeking!"

Smiling indulgently, I do as he asks and now rely on my remaining senses as he leads me along confidently. I feel the soft grass underfoot change into something crispier; something crunchier. I'm thinking maybe we're entering one of the small woodland glades in the park… can smell pine cones, woody aromas, faint scent of barbecue smoke.

"And…. ta-da!" he declares triumphantly, giving my arm a little squeeze. I quickly open my eyes to see a small clearing transformed into our own privately-enclosed restaurant. Two deckchairs and a small table dominate the space over which a canopy of tangled branches and leaves provide a light-speckled ambience. The wooden table is crammed with goodies: tiny sandwiches with the crusts cut off, sausage rolls, fancy cakes and an assortment of crisps… Pride of place - exactly in the centre of the table – are two tumblers and a large glass jug with purplish liquid inside. Colourful orange, lemon and lime slices float enticingly on the surface, but the fluid itself is dark and mysterious, containing secrets and memories within its indistinct depths. Thoughts shared only by the two of us. I look at Matt in wonder: he's remembered – it's just like the song!

Pulling out a deckchair, Matt motions me towards it. "Lunch is served," he says in important tones, placing a crimson napkin carefully on my lap as I sit down. I marvel at the selection of bite-size foods, aimed to tantalise and tempt the appetite without being too overwhelming; he's chosen with care and sensitivity and I love him for that.

We talk. We eat. As the time passes, the sun flickers teasingly in and out of our secluded bistro, varying the stages of atmosphere from startlingly clear hues to enigmatic shadows. And in-between moments where the leaves part in the breeze, give us a quick glimpse of sunbeams and then dance back again in humour. We talk more. Laugh. I can't eat a lot, naturally, but it doesn't matter; the food and drink is just a backdrop for our togetherness. Our time of freedom. Unrestricted by the presence of others and unencumbered by anything but the here and now. Around us, the melodies soar higher and higher, all-encompassing but unobtrusive.

Finally, when I'm beginning to shiver slightly from inactivity, Matt stands and stretches. "Now… time for the second part of our excursion," he says softly, taking my hand and helping me from my deckchair.

I look at him curiously, the song lyrics flitting back into my consciousness. "We're going home already?" I question, my eyes starting to well up in an almost childish disappointment.

He shakes his head, smiling. "No – I'm mixing things around a little, that's all; call it artistic licence if you like. There's more to come, don't worry!"

I laugh with him, relieved. Our perfect day shouldn't be cut short. Not for anything.

"But what about…?" I gesture over to our picnic debris. "Shouldn't we clear all this up first?"

He takes my hand and squeezes it gently. I squirm a little, knowing that it will feel bony; *too* bony. But if he notices, he doesn't mention it. "Nope," he says enigmatically, "It'll all be taken care of; no worries."

We wander away from our picnic to the outskirts of the woods, walking slowly and companionably. Climb into Matt's car –parked nearby - and drive away. I'm not instructed to close my eyes this time so it doesn't take me long to realise where we're destined. After all, Matt doesn't have the capacity to disguise the many signs along the roadside! They're very distinctive signs too; brown with white lettering, adorned with a not so subtle elephant.

"Of course!" I exclaim, grinning happily as we slow down and turn around the winding corner.

"Couldn't be anywhere else," Matt corroborates, pulling smoothly into the wide-gated entrance and buzzing down his window to pay the man in the booth. The old chap grins toothily and winks at us.

"If you hurry, you'll be in time to watch the penguins having their tea," he says conspiratorially. "Sight for sore eyes, that is."

I turn to Matt eagerly. "Shall we?"

He smiles at my enthusiasm. "If that's what madam wishes, then that's what we shall do; first stop penguin enclosure, then."

Naturally, the penguins don't disappoint. The very sight of them rushing around, falling over each other to get to their food, makes us giggle. The keeper asks us if we'd like to don gloves and feed some of the birds by hand, so we do. One particularly chubby female takes a liking to Matt; after satiating herself with fish, she starts to follow him devotedly, beak to leg, at the same time watching me balefully with beady eyes in case I try to interfere. The more Matt tries to lose her, the more persistent she becomes. I stand to one side, shaking with almost hysterical laugher, while he performs a little sort of side-step dance to try to confuse her away from him.

Spotting my mirth he shakes his head then chuckles with me. "You're not helping much, are you?" he moans, finally giving up and stopping still. His admirer barges into him and gives him an approving peck on the shin. "Ow!" he yells, girl-like and shrill. The penguin lifts her head up – puzzled - gives a little chitter of disgust and then waddles back to the pile of dead fish for a concluding snack.

Matt flops down on a nearby bench and rolls his trousers up to inspect the damage. " Reckon that's going to leave a bruise," he mutters, mock-crossly. I sit down too and lean against him, exhausted with my laughing. He puts his arm around me. We spend several moments just sitting, the heat of the sun warming our arms as we hold each other tightly. After a while, Matt tilts my face to his and looks deep into my eyes. "Ok?" he asks quietly.

I nod back at him. Tired but ok, yes. More ok than I've been for months now, to be honest.

"So, shall we move on then?" he says. "I'm sure there are many more animals that would just love to entertain us."

I let him lead me away from the excited chirruping of the penguins and we walk slowly towards the direction of the big cat enclosure. I'm drawn to the disdain and elegance of these haughty creatures who, despite their captivity, seem to emit a sense of freedom in the way they flick their eyes uncaringly at us. Maybe that's the punch line – we are the captives and they the keepers. Emotionally. After all, do they have the anxieties and angst that runs through our veins? I can answer this in less than a second, with an emphatic *no*.

We continue to watch their languid movements for several minutes, admiring their sinuous limbs and glossy coats. They seem totally unaffected by the outside world; I suppose they have everything they need within their own confines and, as long as they don't think about the fact that they *are* confined, life is good. I consider this for a little while, feeling a little removed from my own limitations now. Sotto voce melodies cushioned in a cotton-woolish sensation. A feeling of detachment. Disconnection. I like it.

Time is moving on. I place a hand on Matt's arm. "Shall we do the movie now then? What's it to be – some sort of thriller or adventure film?"

His eyes glint mischievously. "I think you'll be pleasantly surprised," he says confidently as we stroll back to the car. Not a blood and guts choice then today. We haven't seen a film together for ages – years, possibly – but the last one we *did* see was a mixture of supernatural phenomena and gut-wrenching carnage. Not my cup of tea at all. At least he had the decency to apologise for his choice when he noticed my face gradually turning greener and greener. Suggested we left straight away and went for a drink instead.

Intriguingly, Matt is driving us past the huge multiplex cinemas. We're travelling out of town, further and further until we stop outside a small, slightly shabby building. Strange. Looking more closely, I see that it is one of the old-fashioned picture-houses, hosting just one film. The notes in my heart increase in volume and speed as I scan the board outside: 'Brief Encounter.' My all-time favourite film. Beaming, I turn to Matt. "Wow!"

He grins back at me. "I know – they only do a couple of showings a year so it was lucky I read about it in the paper in time for today."

I consider this. "Not so much lucky as that it was meant to be, I think."

But as we enter the dark room, following the usherette's thin torchlight, I realise that Matt has had more to do with the arrangement than simply reading a paper. More than predestination has organised too. We are led, importantly, to the plushest seats in the house, one of which has a colourful bouquet of flowers laid on it. Matt picks these up and presents them to me. "Beautiful flowers for a beautiful lady."

I sit down and bury my nose in their fragrance, feeling, inexplicably, a pang of sadness – a tinge of minor melody interrupting my major key mood. "Thank you; they're lovely." Looking for distractions, I stare around the room; there's not one other person besides us here, apart from the usherette standing by to tend to our needs. Matt follows my gaze. Shrugs. "I thought it'd be nice to have the place to ourselves," he explains. "More intimate."

I smile my thanks and settle in my seat as the haunting chords of Rachmaninoff's Second Piano Concerto announce the beginning of the film. The notes mingle with the song already playing in my heart; gradually overwhelm, leaving it to hover uncertainly in the side-lines, waiting for its chance to reappear. The piano builds up to a crescendo and then rumbles into back into the shadows as the story commences. Immediately, I forsake myself in the ever-popular tale of love. Secure and content with Matt by my side I temporarily disregard – discard, even - who I am, *what* I am.

Some two hours later, when the orchestral notes are only a lingering memory, and the closing credits have finished, my delicate melody begins to ring softly out again, refreshed and lyrical, singing and extending.

I turn to Matt. He is the life force that enables me to 'keep hanging on'; I recognise this truth. That's how I've got this far, with his love and support. We both know that it can't go on for ever. Has to come to an end. But – I look into his eyes and see the love reflected there – perhaps it can now; now that we've had our perfect day.

\*\*\*

Sophie sighs now, sinking down further into the soft warmth of the hospital bed. She feels her heart's fragile rhythm decrease gradually in spirit and beat; falling into rallentando, and then later, diminuendo… As she closes her eyes – now acquiescent – her pulse, slowing beat by beat, falls in time with the end of the song in her heart.

Stops. No regrets…

# 13

# DESTINATION DELAYED

Truthfully, I do feel a bit let down. Mostly at the lack of acknowledgement. I mean, I'd thought your whole life was supposed to flash before you: the best bits, the worst bits, the mediocre bits? And the bright light that's supposed to lead you to… well, Heaven or Hell? Nowhere to be seen. No, I'm distinctly underwhelmed by the whole scenario.

I drift across the ward, quietly waiting. It occurs to me that I'm not feeling exactly as you think you would in this situation. I'd have expected sadness, dejection – at least some kind of regret at shuffling off the old mortal coil. Even an element of confusion, perhaps. Instead, I feel… nothing. Except, of course, a slight pique that there's no angel, etc. to lead me to a better place (*better* being the preferred route, obviously). Then again… perhaps he or she will come later? Maybe they're just running late. Could be. Ok, well, in that case, I'll just hang around and wait. People watch, possibly.

I soon grow bored; there's not a lot of entertainment value in a sly pick of the nose, a surreptitious scratch of the genitals. Even when I eavesdrop on a nurse's whispered phone call to a lover who just happens to be her superior's husband, this too fails to intrigue me.

I sigh and glance up at the large clock. Two fifteen. It's been three hours since my passing. Three houses since, well, my… *body* was removed. But, to be truthful, I'm not really interested in that wrinkled old thing anymore. Fundamentally because the vital part of me is here. *Still* here. And that, of course, is the problem; you'd really think I'd have been on my way by now. I sigh again, trying to cast my now-niggling worries aside. No point in getting riled at this point. It's not in my character to make a fuss. Never has been.

However… I reflect on this paramount aspect of my personality. Maybe it's not so much an endearing feature as a major flaw? Thinking about it, maybe *that's* why no-one has bothered to collect me yet because they know I won't make a fuss about their tardiness. They'd rightly assume that I would meekly ignore any stalling, however lengthy. Bloody cheek! I've had a lifetime of going along with things and even at the *end* of my life I'm still waiting around for decisions to be made for me?

I feel an unfamiliar flicker of anger, like a sleepy phoenix fluttering slowly from a dusty pile of ashes. Why should I hang around here? This is the most important day of my… well, *death*, and here I am just passively waiting. All these years I've gone along with everything that's happened; simmering but never fighting. Right… well… Time for action, methinks - I'm going to do something proactive at last. Yes. But what, exactly? Hmm… Ah… maybe… maybe I'll pay a quick visit to the people who have wronged me: have the last word, as it were. It might be a rather immature idea but actually I really don't care – what can they do, after all? It'll show them – and that bloody procrastinating angel – that Thomas Jackson is *not* to be messed with.

I scan back over my seventy-seven years. Glossing over minor slurs and affronts – I don't know how much time I've got, after all - I focus in only on those events which have really impacted on my life. The first which comes to mind is when I was passed over for promotion. Not *that* bad, you'll say, but, in the end, it turned out to be the only time I had a chance to better myself in the factory. Didn't know that at the time, of course. Neither did I know about the rumours which had prevented me from being promoted. Rumours started by Albert, my former colleague and so-called friend…

Yes – Albert will be my first port of call. But where is he now? And how will I get there? I consider this dilemma for a few seconds before recalling an old TV programme featuring a ghost who could transport himself simply by visualising exactly where he wanted to go. Well… I've nothing to lose. The situation is surreal enough as it is; if this is going to work, today would be the day. I focus in on my old friend and…

Blimey, I'm back in the factory! However, the machines and desks have been shifted to the sides of the large room; large tables filled with buffet food are now in their place and there's some sort of celebration going on. I drift towards the head of the main table, towards the guest of honour: Albert. He's returned to where he first started – back to his starting point on the factory floor. But why? Oh, hold on – I suddenly notice the 'Happy Retirement' banners hanging gaudily from the tables; management must've thought it amusing to have the party in the place where he began his upward spiral to success. Right…

I stare curiously at my former friend. Even though it's been years since we last met - his first promotion was only the start of a series of upgrades in jobs, houses and, unsurprisingly, friends - he's still easy to recognise. Same rather arrogant profile. Haughty demeanour. Plus, he now has a huge stomach and somewhat bloodshot eyes. The good life has obviously taken its toll - ha! Although… and now I feel an unwelcome curdle of envy trickling through me – he is, at least, still alive.

Anyway. Now's my chance to tell him exactly how I feel about his betrayal. I open my mouth to berate him, but nothing happens - I can't speak: I don't exist. Why on earth didn't I realise this would happen? Stupid, stupid, stupid! I begin to float away in abject disappointment. Nothing doing here then. Until a thought occurs… I can't talk but maybe, just maybe…

I stare intently at the space immediately in front of me. Concentrate feverishly for several minutes until - all those supernatural programmes I watched weren't in vain, after all – my hands begin to re-emerge! Still focussing absorbedly, I will them to travel towards a large chocolate gateau sited on the main table and, in fascination and awe of my new powers, lift the cake high. Transport it towards Albert. He blinks, seemingly unable to comprehend what is happening, his lips frozen in mid pompous-anecdote. Finally, he blanches as my hands take the final step and crush the chocolate creation into his flabby face!

Chuckling as much as I can in my new insubstantial state, I feel a huge sense of satisfaction: job well done. I smirk at the bewildered faces around me, then peer upwards, scanning for signs of my angel. Surely *now* it's time? But… nothing. Oh well. I drift towards the ceiling, pondering on my next visitation.

It doesn't take long to decide. Brother George. Again, unseen for ages, right back to around the time Mother died, some twenty years ago. He did *try* to keep in touch – phone calls, occasional visits etc. I was unreceptive to his advances, though, and who could've blamed me, after what I suspected? However, I had no proof, and he being the oldest and the executor of the will meant I couldn't voice my suspicions. Obviously, this soured our relationship from then on. Now I need to see him, however – I need *closure*, as it's popular to say these days.

A moment of concentration and I'm there. After a cursory glance at George – more wrinkled, rather greyer, but basically much the same – I look around his huge living room with interest. He's seated on a comfy sofa, remote control in hand, watching an obscenely large plasma TV. Not the same sparsely furnished two-bed flat where we had our last awkward conversation about Mother's wishes then? No, now he resides in a comfortable Victorian semi, expensively decorated and accessorised. I sigh, returning my gaze back to his face. So there *was* money - I knew it! I *knew* it hadn't all gone on Mother's last days in the care home. The selfish...

I turn back to George. Oblivious to my scrutiny, he's chuckling away at an old Buster Keaton movie on the screen. If he'd taken any money – or, more likely, had found it (Mother wasn't one for banks or building societies) – why couldn't he have shared it between us? It would've made *both* our lives more comfortable in our old age. The unaccustomed anger is back; I feel it making its way slowly through my spirit, searching for an exit from which to vent its wrath. *My* wrath. After deliberation, I reflect on an old prank a colleague told me he once played on his landlord... Perfect. Drifting into the kitchen, I manage – with considerable meditation - to open the huge fridge door. Yes - just what I'm looking for - a plate of kippers. I knew the old codger would still have his favourite snack handy. With comparative ease – I'm getting good at this – I manoeuvre several fish upwards, finally squeezing them into a small opening between sink unit and cupboard. Ah... the sweet smell of success! Smirking, I drift away.

Right. I know exactly where I'm going next and, with the non-presence of my angel, there's no-one to stop me. And, to be honest, in my present motivated state of mind, there's no-one who *could* stop me. Not now. Seconds later, as I waft towards the presence of the two people I haven't seen for the longest time – the two people who I once would've trusted with my life – I know I've made a good choice for my third visitation. Andrew and Jill. My previous – *very* previous - best friend and girlfriend.

As I arrive - absent-mindedly reflecting that this form of transportation is so much more efficient than the consistently late No. 34 – I feel unexpected nerves kick in. More so than the previous two episodes. Probably because this couple's actions caused me the most heartache; a pain which was practically off the scale at the time, and, just like the other occasions, an emotion I really hadn't anticipated. I focus on the couple sitting on the sofa. Smiling into each other's eyes, they're chatting animatedly about... grandchildren? I listen in with interest. Yes; grandson Tom has won a place at a prestigious music college in London. Despite myself, I can't help feeling impressed. Andrew's love of music has obviously been passed down the generations. As they chat, my attention begins to wander a little. I gaze around the room, noting the happy family photos; holidays, christenings, proms... Seems like they've made their relationship work then, despite its inauspicious beginning. I shudder, thinking back to that time. Catching them kissing when I returned home unexpectedly. Tears, recriminations, apologies. Within minutes, me walking away from the two of them, unable to express exactly how I felt but fully aware that this event marked the end of an era; knowing I would no longer have either of these people in my life.

So... my revenge? I hesitate. Needing inspiration, I reach down inside me for the simmering frustration which has been put on hold all this time, only to find that it has dissipated: gone. I'm confused: surely seeing the two of them together would've been the spur I needed to exact a grisly retaliation? But it would seem not; I have nothing inside me that suggests I need or want to destroy their relationship. And even more strangely, part of me seems to be pleased that it worked out for them; at least it proves they were right together: it was meant to be.

Bewildered at my unexpected thoughts, I turn away, preparing to drift elsewhere... *anywhere*. But as I do so, I catch sight of a bright light in the distance, travelling speedily towards me. Is it, could it be... my angel? I squint anxiously into the glow. A warm smile beams back at me, followed by a beckoning gesture. Yes – it is. At last. Relieved, I float towards the light, a sensation of approval and warmth enveloping me as I'm gently embraced. Security and acceptance at last...

# 14

# COMING HOME

## Monday 31st October 1966

It was raining then; it's raining now. I stop walking and peer downhill. To where it used to be. To *what* it used to be. School. The only bit I recognise is the roof; but now it's on the ground with mud and rubble and stuff all around. Waste. Strange word, that. I heard the grown-ups talking about *wasted lives*. But it's *waste* that fell from the mountains. Muddy, mucky, sludgy waste. Slipped down the hills and covered our school. I frown – I still don't really understand how this happened. Or why. No-one has talked to me about it, explained it. Not yet, anyway.

I tuck the small bunch of flowers in my pinafore for safe-keeping so's I can use both hands to clamber downwards. Slip. Slide. As I scramble, I dirty my knees and hands with the black sticky gunge. I don't s'pose it will matter; nothing seems to be important in our house now. Even food. I've had to remind Mam when it's tea-time every day this week, but she just looks at me blankly as if she doesn't know what I mean. I'm not allowed to use the knife – too sharp - so I tear big chunks off the bread with my hands. Get a spoon, spread butter and jam on the slabs and place them in front of her. Look at her hopefully. Sometimes she eats. But mostly she doesn't. It's like she's not there anymore; I mean, I know she *is*, but it feels like she isn't. Almost as if her mind has been taken over by aliens or something. Like those Daleks in the

Doctor Who film we saw a few weeks ago. I hid behind the sofa and only peeked out now and again. But Tommy sat right opposite the TV and watched every single second. Bravely. No fidgeting.

Tommy. That's why I'm here: to give him the flowers. And they're for the others too, of course. But mainly Tommy: my brother. I know I could go to the cemetery but I don't really want to. That's where everyone else goes. There's loads of flowers there; loads of people too, wailing and howling. It doesn't feel like Tommy is there, though. But then I don't know *where* he is, really. The vicar said that all the dead people are in our hearts forever; that they are angels now, up in Heaven. I don't get that – how can they be in Heaven *and* in our hearts? It doesn't make sense. I wish Tommy was here to explain it to me. He was good at that – explaining. Even though he used to pretend that I was a pain when I kept asking him things, I think he liked it really. He liked feeling clever.

I wonder what he'd say to me now. Probably call me a jammy bugger for not being at school the day it all happened. He was cross that I had the day off, even though I had a really snotty cold and Mam had said I should stay at home. But he wasn't happy about that at all. Even said he thought he should stay off too, cos he was sure he was coming down with something. But Mam just laughed and said, "Get off with you lad," smacking his bum as he left the room. He'd only gone upstairs though, cos he soon came back with something under his arm. His Beano annual. Pulled it out and gave it to me. "Here, you can read this if you want, Susie – stop you getting bored today." I'd smiled – I knew how much that book meant to him – but he'd quickly run off before I got a chance to thank him…

I look up now. The rain has finally stopped and the sky's brighter. Clearer. I've reached the edge of the huge hole and I think that's near enough; I don't really want to get any closer. I take out the flowers from my pinafore pocket. They're a little bit squashed but not too much. I don't think Tommy will mind. He wasn't really one for flowers anyway, but flowers are what you bring, aren't they? Tommy didn't really notice that sort of thing, I don't think. Apart from the ones he used to get told off for flattening when he was playing football in the garden. That's where I picked these from – our garden. I couldn't have bought any from a shop cos I haven't had any pocket money for a little while. Over a week now.

I lay the flowers carefully on a big smooth stone. I feel like I should say something now, but I don't really know what. I haven't got the words, somehow. I stroke the petal of one of the blue flowers and think about my brother; I push painfully into my mind to picture his toothy grin and messed-up blond hair. Scabby knees and ink-stained fingers. Loud. Lively. I remember the tricks and pranks he played on me and smile a little, cos he'd laugh about the fact that I'll never get a chance to get my own back now. I slowly stand up and take a deep breath. "Bye Tommy."

### Tuesday 31st October 2006

Sunshine. A light mist across the valley blurs the hills and grasses into Impressionist paint effects, like a well-remembered day dream. I open the car door and re-breathe damp Welsh air, familiar even after all these years. Too many years. A memory inducing ambience, I reflect, as a multitude of sensations flicker and filter through my jet-lagged brain; sensations which evoke the whole emotional spectrum of my childhood. Early memories... Running across the valleys with a whole bunch of children, screaming in pretend fear that I'd be caught and have to be 'it'; taking it in turns to roll down the bumpy grassland, head tucked in and arms folded for speed; walking to school with Tommy, tattered satchel on my back and lunch pail in my hand...

Then later memories; recollections from the bleakest of times. No warning as the light plunged to dark, like a unexpected punch in the solar plexus. And then silence. Silence where there used to be laugher - pulsating, vibrant, *animated* laughter. Followed by bleak confusion. Despair... Leaning on the car I close my eyes, remembering the disorientated child that I was back then. Desolate. But I need to pull myself together – to get a grip. *I can do this.* So I blink my tears back, take a breath and retrieve my old hessian bag from the car. Check to make sure that the precious item is still there; drawing it out and running my fingers over the smooth surface. Right.

I slam the car door decisively and begin to walk. Slow, steady footsteps. I know where I'm going. Have confidence in finding my way, even after all these years. Of course, I'm not in totally unfamiliar territory - Mam used to send me photos as the site developed, so I vaguely recognise the path, the signs, the trees, but even if she hadn't, I would still have been able to find my way. Instinctively.

As I walk, I reflect that even now as an adult, I have no wish to visit the cemetery; on returning to my home country, I still don't feel any affinity with the rows and arches of white stone that denote our catastrophe and keep guard over our dead. No. I've thought about this; thought about it carefully. I want to go back to where it happened – I want to go back to our school. So I follow the pathway purposefully. Down towards the Memorial garden. I remember some of Mam's weekly phone calls years ago, telling me of the plans to re-design the area. Commemorating the 25th anniversary. Finally, they'd asked what the families wanted to see there. And - in response - reduced the high walls so visitors could marvel at the awe-inspiring views up and down the valley. Planted hopeful young saplings. Grown blue and pink blooms to represent all of the boys and girls who had lost their lives...

On approaching the entrance to the carefully landscaped gardens, I pause, noticing that Nature herself has had more than a tentative hand in the organising and planting here. As well as the carefully structured arrangement of brightly-coloured flowers and shrubs, there are flashes of wild flowers breaking up the formal positioning; adding a cheeky mischievousness to the overall effect. I smile, fancying that maybe my tatty bunch of wild flowers had a little input with these decorations; maybe their great-great-great-great forebears...

A proud and upright foxglove catches my eye. Standing tall in a mixture of smaller, frailer plants, it reminds me of our old Deputy Head in the playground, watching over the smaller, more delicate children and making sure they didn't get knocked over in the rough and tumble ball games of the older children. I nod to myself; yes. And those little white, pink and red cornflowers are like the infants – delicate, small and with the potential to be knocked over by the slightest breeze.

But not Tommy – definitely not! He would be the windflower, feisty and inventive; not afraid to go his own way and make his own choices, whether they proved right or wrong. I walk over now to the Tommy flower and sit down on the low wall by his side. I tell him all about his nephew – little Tommy – and how he loves football, just like his namesake. I tell him of my son's fascination with history and his particular interest in genealogy. How, despite living hundreds of miles away, he loves to Skype his Nana in Wales and talk to her about his relatives, past and present. How he begged to come along with me. But I'd put him off and told him he needed to stay and look after his Dad and little sister. I needed to make the journey by myself. This time.

I fumble in my bag and retrieve the old Beano annual from the depths of the hessian. Bending down, I place the book in a crevice of the low stone wall, and then straighten, gazing up at the cloudless blue sky. I'm aware of a wisp of serenity hovering above me; after a few seconds, it stills and then finally swoops downwards. Seeps into my heart. Soothing. Comforting. I take a deep breath before I speak and let the words float and then soar into the afternoon sky. "Thank you for being my brother."

*Any similarity to names of those involved in the disaster is purely coincidental. Although based on real events this story is an entirely fictional account.*

# 15
# AFTER THE EVENT

Eventually, the word I'd been searching for tumbled into my thoughts. I rolled it around a little and then - cautiously – gave it a voice: "Compunction." Only just adequate really. With the absence of anything better, I left it there on my tongue, spreading spongily into my fissures and slowly soaking my inner core. Then stared down at the bulk on the floor, preparing to fasten the word to this gently leaking form. Failed.

It was too soon, of course. Had I not been experiencing this strange mixture of euphoria and incredulity, I would have recognised that now was not the time for classification. After all, what was done was done. No amount of wordsmithery would change things. Instead, I should have been focussing on the practicalities: specifically, what to do about… it.

Time to act. I sighed, the breath exceptionally loud in my reproachful kitchen. Right… So… Procrastinating just a little more, I gave the body a little nudge with the tip of my shoe. Just to see. Nothing. Well, in honesty, I don't know exactly what I was expecting, but…

Ok. I glanced around the room looking for possible disposal insight. After all, with no premeditation, I had nothing ready to facilitate the aftermath of my deed. Nothing. Surely there had to be something I could use? Bin liners? No - not strong enough. Boxes? Frowning, I reflected on my activity yesterday – I try to keep myself busy; it helps a little - packing up and delivering my old books to the charity shop. In boxes. Not boxes then.

My eyes turned to the large stainless steel bin in the corner: would that be big enough? Possibly. However, in order to be certain, I would have to get close to it, manipulate; touch...

The alternative? Well, that was simpler in some ways: grab my mobile and admit the deed. Punch in three numbers and someone else would deal with the scenario: the blood, the carnage, the disarray. Convenient. However, I'd then have to explain. Be held accountable for my actions.

I know some would understand; those who had flinched at my black eyes, tutted at bruised arms, questioned my reluctance to accept invitations. But the others: the people who didn't know me? Would they think: why didn't she just leave him? Why resort to this? As if I'd planned it. No, I was sure they wouldn't empathise with the white-hot rage that had suddenly flooded my previously numbed mind, like the rush-back of a tsunami after withdrawal. They wouldn't comprehend how someone could retaliate so violently after decades of submission.

However, I digress. A decision has to be made. And finally realising I can't – won't – be able to physically dispose of my misdemeanour, I sigh and pick up my mobile. Make the call.

***

Compunction. Of course you could say that it's too little, too late; the deed already having been done. You could. But there I'd have to disagree: surely any type of regret is better than none? For the record, yes, I do lament my actions. But perhaps my sorrow is not quite as it should be, for I merely regret not doing the deed sooner. Years ago, in fact.

# 16
# BINGO

"Another lucky winner!" Matron boomed, wobbling over to Ethel and placing the tin of chocolate biscuits on her lap. "Well, that's it for today, folks, but we'll have another exciting game next week – same time, same place." She began to pick up the tatty bingo boards adorning the resident's laps, tutting quietly at the inaccurate placing of many of the counters.

Albert looked at George, raising one grey eyebrow and clacking his teeth in exasperation. "Exciting?" he muttered sourly, "I've had more excitement putting the breadcrumbs out for the birds. Humph!" He rose stiffly to his feet, dotting and stabbing his cane stick into a satisfactory position before slowly making his way out of the large sitting room.

George nodded belatedly, watching his friend's unsteady progress and wondering whether tea and biscuits would be forthcoming now that the bingo had finished. A custard cream would be just the thing at this stage of the afternoon, especially as it was still over an hour until teatime. He peered round hopefully at Ethel, the winner, registering disappointedly that she had now fallen asleep, her arthritic hands curled around the unopened tin of biscuits. A thin and wavering line of saliva filtered down her whiskery chin, looking like a slime trail belonging to a confused slug. George sighed and let his eyes drift over to the TV instead.

***

Sometime later, after dinner, George and Albert were back in their favoured positions by the window. To members of staff, they maintained that this particular location enabled them to study the – meagre – number of birds which visited the front garden, but actually (as all the employees knew) they were surveying the number of 'outsiders' who came to visit their ageing relatives. Sometimes, in a particularly dull week, the pair might place a small bet on who would receive the most visitors, although, as Matron had advised in the last staff meeting, this was not to be encouraged as it would often result in the old men having 'words' or – even worse - 'silences'. Still, to George and Albert, this pastime whiled away some of the hours; hours which were otherwise filled with the unproductive sound of snoring and the faint smell of – on a good day - disinfectant.

Now, noticing his companion's red-veined eyelids beginning to droop, Albert reached laboriously for his cane and poked George firmly in the ribs. "Ahem," he began, in a too-loud proclamation, feeling aggrieved at being the only one awake in the stifling morgue of a lounge.

George startled, easing his blue-filmed eyes back open again. "What?" he responded grumpily; he didn't appreciate being poked, especially with all the weight he'd lost in the last few years: it hurt.

Albert straightened slightly in his chair, assuming an air of formality. "This weekly bingo travesty we have to put up with…"

"What about it?" George wasn't really in the mood for chatting and would've been quite content to doze until it was time for bed, if left to his own devices. But it wasn't to be – now he'd got the other man's attention, Albert was determined to persevere.

"It's bloody boring – that's what!" Using his cane, Albert gestured derisively around the room, allowing the point to linger momentarily upon each slumbering resident. "Look at them all; just look!"

George looked. And, upon looking, he had to privately concede that, for most of the elderly people, it wasn't their finest hour. In various stages of apathy, they sprawled, curled and gaped around the room, emitting little noises of post-mastication bliss, distress or confusion (depending on the individual)

Seeing the comprehension in George's eyes, Albert continued - at last he had the other man's attention. "Living here doesn't have to be like this, you know – we don't *have* to be bored and… and *boiled* into submission!"

George nodded. He had found from past experience that when Albert got into this mood it was normally just best to let him rant on until he tired himself out. Obviously, the occasional word of agreement or consolation was needed at a decent interval, but that was usually all that was required. "Mmm," he responded carefully, allowing a thoughtful expression to settle upon his deeply lined face.

"So that got me thinking – well, that bloody Bingo was the last straw, to be honest." Albert shook his grey head incredulously. "I mean… if that's all they can come up with to keep us entertained, we may as well go to our graves now; death can't be any less exciting than the prospect of winning a tin of biscuits." At this, he spat contemptuously onto the windowsill but then, suddenly remembering, looked around anxiously to make sure Matron wasn't nearby. She didn't approve of spitting –

totally unhygienic, she declared – and could be quite acerbic in her chastisements.

Despite his reservations, George felt he had to be fair to the nursing home – to a certain degree. "Last week it *was* a box of chocolates," he ventured hesitantly. "And once, I think I remember it being a- a bottle of booze." He paused and scratched his grizzled chin thoughtfully. "Although, on reflection, it may have been non-alcoholic; yes, that was it - non-alcoholic beer."

Albert threw him a disparaging look. "Exactly!" he scoffed, gallantly resisting the urge to spit once more. "So, I'm sitting in my room, thinking about our problem… how we can liven up this place, well, even just keep people awake really, and I come up with an idea…"

"Ah," George mumbled. "An idea…" He thought his tone was just encouraging enough – not too interested yet not dismissive either.

"And - this might surprise you – the idea is still based around Bingo. However, this particular bingo would be a game with a difference." Albert settled back smugly in his high-backed chair, waiting for a dramatic reaction from George. However, George continued to stare at him, mystified. Clicking his tongue against his teeth in frustration, Albert persisted nevertheless. "I know what you're thinking – the difference will just be better prizes or even money as winnings but no – that's not it."

George found his voice. "So, what is it then?"

"Aha, well…" With difficulty, Albert manoeuvred himself nearer to the other man's 'good' ear, ignoring the slight whiff of baked beans which emanated from George's grubby shirt collar. "In our Bingo, the stakes will be higher – much higher; we will be playing in terms of… life or death!" He shifted back to his original position, this time gratified with George's horrified response.

"But why... I mean... *how...*?" George stuttered, not entirely sure whether Albert was serious or not.

Albert raised his eyes to the heavens. "Think about it, George – how much longer have we got before we shuffle off this mortal coil, hmm? Probably not even years – months most likely." He threw out his arms as far as his rheumatism would let him (admittedly, this was not as far as he would have liked) "And *this* is all we have to look forward to – *this* and then more of *this!* Not a lot of point really, is there?"

George grunted non-committedly, feeling a small prickle of unease finger his spine.

"So, why not throw caution to the wind, allow a little adrenalin to fizz up our veins and take a few risks, eh?" Albert gave a small laugh, then suddenly remembered a TV programme he'd watched the day before. "Be like one of those radical sports – no, wait, that's not right! *Extreme* – that's it: *extreme bingo!"*

George was slowly catching on. "You're saying that the losers of the game will have to die...? B-but..."

"No, it will be only one person that dies – well, one per game – the winner. And therein lies the twist." Albert was impatient, beginning to tap his cane on the carpeted floor animatedly. "If you win, you have to top yourself. Simple!"

"So the winner will be the person left at the end of a series of games?" George wasn't totally sure that *anyone* would be a winner in these circumstances, but he had to check, just to be sure.

Albert was unconcerned about the technicalities. "Winner, loser, there's no difference really, is there? We've all got to go sometime and at least this way we go with a bit of style – panache, if you like. Break the apathy of our remaining days." He smiled in rather a disconcerting manner, George thought. "Right, so now we have some players to recruit…"

***

A mere few days later - Albert didn't want to take any chances of a chosen one dying of natural causes and missing this opportunity – the four bingo players were sitting around the small table in his bedroom. Albert's system for choosing players had been simple, as he had explained to George the day before. He would solicit anyone over the age of eighty that:

a.  Still had a certain amount of mental capacity *or*
b.  Was suffering from a terminal illness *or*
c.  Didn't have much in the way of interested relatives

George, who had felt rather miffed that he had been *told* rather than *asked* to play, had to concede – grudgingly - that it was a neat way of organising the cast list. Despite his rancour, he began to feel something he hadn't felt for some years and couldn't immediately identify. After a few moments, he came up with… *expectancy.*

Ideally, of course, mused Albert, glancing around at the other three octogenarians, the perfect player would have all three of his requirements. Sadly, Connie was the only one who fitted the bill exactly. Still… Albert felt a thrill of adrenalin running through his veins as he handed out the small Bingo boards; it should be a good game, regardless.

Small, delicate Mabel took her Bingo board with shaking fingers. "This idea of yours certainly trounces Matron's efforts at entertainment," she remarked, gazing at Albert with new admiration. "But, of course, it is quite, *quite* unorthodox."

Albert smiled ingratiatingly and allotted her twenty red counters. "Naturally," he clarified, granting her a gentle pat on the hand, "Surely you wouldn't expect anything less?"

Across the table, Connie also turned to face Albert, giggling girlishly - the tinkling sound quite at odds with her dry, deteriorating body. "Obviously we wouldn't," she chuckled, "Trust you to find a way of returning a certain amount of stress to our advancing years."

Listening to them, George rolled his eyes then picked up his counters. He muttered, "Are we playing, or what?"

***

The first few calls were uneventful with the cheap battery-operated machine 'borrowed' from the office equally allotting two or three numbers to each player. Albert made sure that everyone was shown the arriving ball, lest he be accused of cheating, but the other three were quite content to let him organise things. He was the mastermind of the game, after all. For a while, the only cause of unease was the thought of being caught making their own entertainment; they knew that Matron wouldn't look kindly upon them forming a little clique, and would certainly *not* condone the elected 'prize'.

Before long, however, the four residents forgot their concerns and settled down, happily mocking Albert's bingo calls of 'sticks eleven', 'feeling blue, number two' and suchlike whenever a ball arrived at the top of the machine. It must have been about half an hour into the game when Connie suddenly realised, with a tremulous shiver, that she had only one number left to fill a horizontal line. She glanced at the other boards, not exactly sure what she was hoping to see, and observed that the other three players needed at least two more numbers to fill a line. "So," she ventured aloud, "This could be it." She was pleased to note that her voice was unwavering and clear; for some reason, it was important to her that she didn't appear nervous.

Albert glanced at her and - stiffly - winked. "Ready?" he said, flicking the activate button. "Here we have… dentures alive – number five."

Connie's finger, poised to cover her remaining number – six – made an involuntary shudder and she drew her hand back onto her lap in, in… relief…? disappointment…? She couldn't quite decide. She fiddled with her hearing aid and then turned her undivided attention back to the plastic machine.

"The next number is… "Albert paused for dramatic effect, "Deathly fix – number six." He looked shrewdly at Connie, tapping her papery hand in case she hadn't grasped the significance. "That's you, my lovely."

Connie completed her line decisively with the small counter and glanced around at the others. Her beatific expression was hard to interpret. "Yes, that's me alright – finished."

George removed his counters carefully before turning to Connie, his eyebrows raised slightly. "*How* are you… I mean, *are* you…?" He left the question incomplete, not entirely sure how to phrase it.

Connie shrugged. "Pills, I suppose… Yes – an overdose. It won't be difficult – Matron leaves the trolley unattended in the corridor every morning so I can easily help myself." She shrugged her bony shoulders indifferently. "It's not as if I hadn't thought of it before."

Albert was impressed with her detachment. He stretched stiffly and slowly rose to his feet. "So… same time next week for the rest of us then, I presume?"

***

Days later, as the three members reconvened in Albert's small bedroom, George observed that there was now an air of gravitas to the proceedings. Perhaps, he thought, it was that they were now aware that this was not just a game anymore. Connie had laid down the gauntlet, so they were obliged to follow her lead. Stoically accept their fate. Likewise, as the game proceeded, so too did the intensity in the room. Mabel and George had already excused themselves twice – respectively - to visit Albert's small ensuite, their feeble bladders responding to the tension as they watched the brightly coloured balls bobbing up and down in the plastic machine. Only Albert seemed to be his truculent self, seeming disconnected from the game as if - win or lose, live or die - it made no difference.

They had been playing for well over an hour and had reached the stage where every player needed one more number to complete a line. The nervous conversation from the beginning of the session had petered out and all that now could be heard was the click-click of the machine as it faithfully delivered its coloured balls. With each spherical arrival, Albert paused slightly before announcing the number, almost as if he were enjoying the anticipation of the moment just a little too much. "And the next number is… a flea in Heaven – thirty-seven!"

There was a tiny pause before Mabel covered her final number with a blue counter and quietly murmured, "Ah… I mean – Bingo…" Her brown eyes glazed as her mind drifted to contemplations of starvation and dehydration; these were, she considered, the least invasive methods and could be tolerated reasonably well in the circumstances.

Nodding in satisfaction, Albert began to put away the counters and boards before turning to George and saying jovially, "Just us men now then."

\*\*\*

The next few days passed remarkably quickly for both George and Albert. Certainly, the hours seemed to speed by in a way they never had before during their time in the home. Eventually the day of the final game emerged and the two men met again in the same bedroom. Albert faced George across the table and gave him a slow appraising stare before placing the bingo boards in front of each of them. George gazed back nervously, fingering the thin blue envelope in his trouser pocket. It had arrived the day before and he must have read it at least ten times, constantly smoothing it out, unfolding and folding it. He wasn't sure what to do... It would all depend on the outcome of this game really; if it went his way then there would be no need to say anything, but if it didn't... He decided to wait and see – after all, he would know in a matter of minutes...

It was obvious that Albert was winning - or not - depending on how you interpreted the situation. He had only random squares covered on his board - no suggestion of the beginnings of a line - whereas George was uncomfortably close to completing a vertical column, with only two numbers needed. Feeling tiny beads of sweat materialise over his forehead, George placed his penultimate counter on 'Key to the tomb – twenty-one.' So this was how it was – just one to go – and he knew, just *knew* it was going to be next...

"Heaven's gate – seventy-eight!" called Albert triumphantly, shooting George a victorious glance. George closed his eyes in acquiescence and gave a long, drawn-out sigh.

"What is it?" asked Albert suspiciously. "I hope you're not thinking of trying to back out?"

Opening his eyes to the other man's frown, George finally let go of any hope of Albert understanding that priorities had now changed. Since the letter had arrived yesterday, George had realised that he wanted to live – he *wanted* to accept the invitation and visit his granddaughter and her family in New Zealand. But Albert would never let him renege on the deal – not while he still had breath in his body. *Breath...* George's eyes shifted away from Albert's piercing stare and drifted instead across to the sideboard. The medicine on the sideboard. Albert's lung condition medication. Despite Matron's misgivings, he insisted that the medication couldn't be locked away with the other prescriptions – he *had* to store it in his room.

"No..." said George belatedly, a small gem of an idea forming in his mind. "Of course not."

***

Confidently, with only a quick backward glance at Matron waving anxiously from the airport lounge window, George stepped onto the plane, carelessly tossing his eighty-one years aside like a redundant plastic carrier bag. As he took his seat, a phrase from his schooldays came back to him unexpectedly. "The worm has turned," he said softly to himself, liking the way the words rolled over his dentures. "Yes - the worm has most definitely turned."

# 17
# SURGE

Grey flakes land gently on my hands as I knead the dough, taking me by surprise. Ash? Pausing in my work, I glance across to the open doorway, looking for an explanation. But I find no justification: no response. Around me, my colleagues continue to labour, seemingly unperturbed by the sprinkling of feather-light matter invading our workplace. It is just an accompaniment to the small vibrations which have now been rumbling for the past two days. Tremors, of course, are usual – an everyday part of life here. But this – this... *substance* is something new: rare. And the two elements together feel wrong. Very wrong.

Ignoring scowls from the others – *the bread still needs to be made* – I step out into the courtyard and lift my eyes to the now darkening sky. Earlier, the sun had tiptoed and danced through morning and now, at the hottest hour, should be satiating our town in golden splendour. Presently, only the thinnest thread of light is penetrating the escalating whirl of powdery flakes, and even this is waning, receding with a whimper to be devoured into the greyish mass. I raise a hand and shade my eyes in trying to locate the source of the deluge, finally tracing it to the looming shape above. Mount Vesuvius. I frown. This can't possibly be the onset of eruption: the geographer Strabo has confidently stated that the volcano is extinct. Dead. Has been for several centuries. And yet... I continue to stare upwards, causing several stallholders in the street to follow my gaze. Duplicate my actions.

Vesuvius, as ever, stands proud; the impenetrable onlooker of our town - steadfast and unchanged. But I shiver slightly as I continue to watch, recognising that this description is not true of her today; *today* she seems to have thrown aside her guardian role and instead taken on the mantle of leash-straining beast, desperate to be set free. Rumbling, grumbling, hissing, spitting. Her previously inanimate consistency has awoken into a sentient, pent-up creature of destruction, pre-warned us with the toxic miasma seeping from her core. An omen? But of what?

Lowering my gaze, I gauge the reactions of my fellow citizens. Some are beginning to pack up their wares, presumably aiming to go back to their homes and loved ones. Some stare upwards in silence, heads to one side; determining whether to stay or leave. Retreat or wait. Others speculate and deliberate amongst themselves, with urgent, high-pitched voices and expansive gestures. As we play out our concerns, the ground around us is steadily covered with the fine, silky residue falling from the skies, providing an eerie and colourless backdrop to our apprehension.

After some time standing and watching – I'm not sure exactly how long - I return to the bakery. In here, industry has ceased and my colleagues are gathering up their belongings, like warriors collecting their weapons in preparation for battle: a silent but determined hive of activity. I approach my friend – Quintus – as he makes to leave. "You're going home?"

He nods and then takes hold of my arm. "Marcus, you're welcome to come with me - shelter at my house until we know what's happening."

I think about this; it's true that my house is the furthest away of all the bakers who work here. Coincidentally, it's also the closest to Vesuvius – not that this fact has bothered me before. Not when it was merely a spectre to our everyday life. Now, well… it would take some time to get back home and I'd be travelling right into the heart of the ash residue. I *could* go with Quintus. But then, I reason, I would have just the same chance staying here at the bakery. Better, perhaps, because this is an old and well-structured building, partially protected by the other shops around. I decline his offer with thanks.

With my colleagues having left, I settle down in a corner of the old bakery to wait until such time that the residue lessens and ceases. Despite my anxiety, I'm lulled into dreams and visions stimulated by my odd cocoon-like surroundings. I don't know how many hours pass before, eventually, another sound pierces that of the falling debris: a roar, more urgent and decisive, and similar to the distant rushing of a waterfall. I stumble to the door and cautiously ease it open. Blink as my vision is accosted by the huge mountain before me. No longer is she part of the background scenery; now she dominates the landscape, with sides scaled with fire like the issue from a proud and majestic dragon: reds and oranges and yellows adorning and rolling in ribbons, twirling and twisting, threading and thickening. And - most significantly – travelling: travelling towards our town.

Mesmerised, I stand and stare, initially unable to comprehend the magnitude of what is happening, but then - in sudden decision - I turn from the doorway and begin to run, run away from the increasingly rapid rolling mass of heat. I mingle with the panicking crowd who, emerging from the fragile 'shelters' of their houses, are stumbling their way through abandoned goods and animals in the streets. Screaming. Shouting. Pushing. Shoving. The fear speeds our heartbeats and loosens our inhibitions as, animal-like, we compete in the ultimate race for life.

At odds with my archaic adrenalin swell, I'm suddenly – inexplicably – infused with the spreading realisation that no human could ever out-run this unquenchable devil. Not me, not my compatriots. Not anyone. It's impossible. The thought stifles my brain, spreads down my body and slows my inadequate feet. And so, midst violent jostling and fleeting incredulous expressions, I stop. Motionless. For, if I cannot escape my foe, I will face her instead – man to beast. I turn around and lift my head defiantly. Watch as the blistering surge slithers closer – ever closer – and prepare myself for submersion.

# 18
# CHICKEN RUN

"Chickens?" Rob frowned. He appeared not to have heard the word before. Or at any rate, if he had, there'd obviously been a delay in informing his face.

Kate sniggered, then immediately - and expertly - turned her response into a cough. The last thing she wanted to do was act like some giddy schoolgirl - not at the age of 49, anyhow. Gone were the days of winning her husband round with feminine guile, that was for sure. When she replied, her voice was weary. Resigned, even. "Why not? We've certainly got the space."

"Yes, but… *chickens*? Messy, beady-eyed, *squawking* creatures." Rob sighed heavily. "Well, I suppose there's no point in me giving you my opinion on this – you're obviously going to go through with it, regardless of what I say." The 'as usual' hung in the air between them, like an angry gnat biding time before attacking a particularly tender area of flesh. The couple stared at each other for a moment before Rob shook his head, scratched his stubbly chin and moved over to the kettle, flicking the switch on aggressively. The conversation seemed to be over.

Kate, resisting the urge to give his disapproving back the finger, instead fished out a tatty piece of paper from her jeans pocket. Smoothing it down on the worktop, she re-checked her list: wood, nails, wire, hardboard… She paused. Considered. That should be all she needed to build a coop, surely? It wasn't as if chickens needed an elaborate dwelling place, after all. Just a sort of hut construction, with a pen leading off from it for them to peck the ground and all those other chicken-y things that they liked to do. Yes, that was fine. She grabbed her bag and made for the door, intent on leaving for B and Q before any family hangers-on spotted her departure and demanded to come too.

An hour or so later, she stood in her back garden, surrounded by piles of wood and wire. She frowned down at her mobile. "Simple?" she muttered, turning the phone this way then that. "How can it be simple if you can't even tell which way up it goes?" With a snort, she threw the offending article into a clump of daisies. Snatched up a couple of the planks. "Right, I'll create it without instructions - how hard can it be? And without help too; I haven't needed a man for a good few years, after all."

She began to line up the pieces of wood in height order, appraising them with a deliberate air of confidence. Nodded to herself. "Ok. The tallest planks will be the supporting posts, then I'll attach them to each other with the slightly shorter ones. Yes, and then the hardwood in between them, to block out the draughts…"

As she positioned the poles, Karen was aware of distant shouting then screaming coming from inside the house. She sat back on her haunches, vaguely wondering at her lack of concern; usually she'd be in the midst of these weekend homework/bath/tidying up rows. But not today. No, out here she felt it really wasn't anything to do with her. At all. Her job was to build this chicken coop and that's what she needed to focus on. A small smile curved her lips as she resumed working again.

Sometime later – she wasn't sure exactly when – she

was surprised to find the sky was darkening. She sighed, muttering, "Damn." She stood and stretched, looking at the construction so far. The erection looked pretty good, even to her critical eyes. *A phoenix rising from the ashes* was the phrase which occurred to her - she wasn't entirely sure why.

Anyhow. She sighed, hoping that, upon returning indoors, she could grab a quick shower and something to eat without any whining or moaning from anyone. After that, she fancied browsing the internet for various frontage ideas for the nearside of the coop. After all, she might as well build a chicken run that was aesthetically pleasing as well as functional...

Over the next few days, having made excuses to her boss -"A nasty flu bug, I really don't know when I'll be back" - and numerous trips to B and Q, Kate was content with the way the project was progressing. Now twice the size of her original idea, she'd determined to make the coop a real home from home. Well, in fact, it was *better* than home, she concluded with some surprise at the end of one particularly industrious day, gazing around at the pastel-coloured walls, the array of cushions arranged on comfy benches and the CD player blasting out her favourite tracks from Madness (Rob always scoffed if she played it indoors) She'd even bought a little electric heater, which was at the moment blazing warmly, courtesy of the long extension lead running from the kitchen. Yes, this was definitely a place to be proud of.

Her smile faded as she became aware of heavy footsteps on the garden path behind her. She turned to see Rob gaping at her construction.

She'd never heard his voice so shrill before. "It's bloody huge! Did you get the measurements wrong?"

Kate met his eyes. Spoke firmly. "Nope. This is exactly the size I planned."

Rob shook his head vigorously. "You're obsessed, woman – ever since you started this you've had no time for the family, the housework – anything. You may as well move into it for the time you've spent making it!"

"Move out here?" Kate raised her eyebrows. Hmm, when she thought about this, it didn't seem such a bad idea. She had felt so much calmer since she'd started making the coop. Motivated. Fulfilled too. And how cosy was the building, now that it was finished? It was a little cocoon of tranquillity: no mess, no noise, no arguments. Sod the chickens, she *could* quite easily live out here. By herself. Happily. "Yes," she concluded, smiling. "This *will* be my new home. Brilliant idea, Rob."

# 19
# THE BEACH HUT

Walking across the beach, Lucy smiled, realising she was counting down the huts in the same way that she had as a child - not in numbers, but in colours: pink, blue, yellow, green; pink, blue, yellow… When she got to the fifth sequence, she slowed her pace. Stopped counting. Yes, it was still there; the last blue in the pastel procession. *Her* hut.

She scrutinised the exterior objectively. It was looking shabby, *very* shabby; it hadn't been treated to a fresh coat of paint for a while, possibly not since they'd last visited – years and years ago. You'd expect a certain amount of deterioration though, taking into account the daily dose of salt air, sun or rain, depending on the weather's whim. Even here on the south coast.

She walked slowly up to the wooden door and inserted the large dull-brass key. Held her breath and turned it, needing to use both hands and all her strength. Stiff. Instinctively, she edged the door upwards a little - just like her dad had shown her all those years ago - and shoved hard. She was in. A musky, salty smell greeted her; a result of the room being unaired, certainly, but in the midst of this she could still make out essence of beach hut – the tangy aroma of holiday.

Leaving the door ajar, she sat down on one of the small wooden chairs and gazed around, her mind suddenly awhirl with memories. The beach hut. It had been her favourite place when she was a child; the one place where rules and regulations were forgotten as soon as the wooden door was eased open. The three children would throw off their clothes, leaving them abandoned on the floor, and quickly pull on their bathing costumes. Buckets, rubber rings and spades were grabbed and it was a race to see who could get onto the beach first. Lucy smiled; it was usually David who won. He had an innate boy's competitiveness that she and Beth didn't really share but were happy enough to indulge him in. They'd all shriek with laughter as they dodged the other holiday-makers on the sands in their inelegant slalom down to the waves. Then that first dip of toe into water. Always colder than she expected, she thought now, with a shiver...

Lucy sighed and gently shook her recollections to one side. This wasn't getting the clearing out done, was it? Right: now to work. She glanced around the room, undecided on where to start. Even though it was a relatively small space – possibly four metres square - it was crammed with paraphernalia as it had been thirty years ago. Like a time capsule preserved for spectators to exclaim and nod sagely over. An eclectic mix of seventies memorabilia. You would've thought someone might have come before now and packed up all the clutter – given some of it away to charity shops, maybe... But then, *who*, exactly? She bit her lip, recollecting how neither she nor her siblings had felt up to the task; not directly after the accident, nor in the years since... After all, it wasn't a job that *had* to be done straight away, not like the house... So the hut had remained as they had last left it: a chaotic, happy snapshot of holiday life. Until now, when she had finally found the strength to come back.

Resolutely, Lucy picked up an empty carrier and

began piling some of the smaller objects into it: shells, pebbles, a craggy string of seaweed... Once the bag was filled, she looked around for something sturdier to hold the buckets, spades, and – she wrinkled her nose in disgust – a couple of stiffened and mouldy beach towels. She eventually located an army-type haversack fit for the purpose and unceremoniously bundled the items into it. There - at least you could now see the floor.

Turning away, intent on her next task, her eyes fell on the old camp bed they'd used for sitting on to play Snap or Twist if the weather had turned rainy and they'd been forced inside. Hmm, it wasn't in bad condition; maybe the kids could use it when their friends stayed over? She bent down and peered underneath the bed, frowning slightly at the clumps of dust and clutter: sweet wrappers, tissues and... a photograph? Yes: an old Polaroid. Lucy picked it up, smoothing it out carefully as she gazed at the young man in the picture, her heart beginning to race. *Jake.* Smiling and carefree, his blond hair messily flicked and his blue eyes sparkling. She began to trace her finger gently over his features, remembering...

He'd been jogging along the beach the first time she'd seen him. A fleeting glimpse - a grin - then he'd sprinted on, leaving her flushed and shy. But he'd come back the next day. Stopped this time for a chat. Then the following day, and the next... Her parents hadn't minded her including Jake in their holidays - *the more the merrier* was their mantra - and had involved him day to day, just as if he were another of their children. But he'd not been a child, of course; he'd been nearly sixteen that first summer, and she'd been fourteen and a half. Neither a child nor an adult. But mature enough to know that she'd found someone special; someone she felt at ease with, someone she could be herself with. Every year, as they reunited on the seashore, ready to take up where they'd left off, her feelings grew stronger and stronger.

*Jake.* Lucy smiled along with the photo as she recalled how safe he'd made her feel, his arm slung along her shoulder as they strolled along the beach. *Like an old married couple* her father had often joked. But then other times they'd just been two kids messing around with buckets and spades. Once, they'd vowed to create the biggest and best sandcastle ever. Had worked all day, digging and positioning sand, patting it carefully into place. The resulting construction had certainly been the biggest she'd ever seen; Lucy still had a vivid image of the turrets standing tall and proud, earning the admiration of all who walked by. Until the tide returned, of course, destroying their hard work effortlessly with one swipe of its watery eraser.

Lucy frowned, her thoughts reflecting on that time - the end of that particular summer: the last summer, as it had turned out to be. Jake had been as full of vigour as ever – more so, really, as he was due to fly out to Australia in a couple of weeks with his brother, working his way around the country for a year or so, maybe more, depending on how it went. And Lucy, well, she'd gained her four 'A' levels and won her coveted place at Oxford; scheduled to start in October. Two paths. Two people that had briefly crossed in life but were now set in different directions. That's how she put it to him, anyhow, foreseeing the end long before he did. But he'd frowned. Shook his head.

"I don't see why you can't come out to visit me in the holidays," he'd insisted, stroking her arm gently. "And I'll come back regularly too. We can still make it work, I know we can!"

Lucy had shaken him off, still angry that he'd honoured the commitment to his brother without even consulting her. "Hardly," she'd stated, moving away from him. "If we'd been in the same country then perhaps, but with you the other side of the world… Well, it's probably best we just make a clean break."

She shuddered now at the immovable teenager she had been. No compromise, no negotiation. It was hardly any wonder that Jake had given up eventually, sad and confused. Left the country with barely a backward glance. And she'd flounced off to Oxford, determined not to let herself be swayed by love again. Thrown herself into her studies, only surfacing at the end of the three years, albeit with a first-class maths degree. And now? Well, the hurt that she'd felt then, the feeling that part of her was missing, had never quite been forgotten but time - if not exactly being a great healer – had helped a little.

She startled at a sudden movement and looked up as a familiar face peered around the open door. *Jake.*

"Couldn't let you sort it all out by yourself, hun, so I blagged some time off work so I could help." Jake gazed around, eyebrows raised. "Not that it seems you've got very far, though!"

Lucy smiled and made a space on the camp bed for him to sit down beside her. "I know, but that's the trouble with revisiting your past: it's time consuming."

Jake laughed and then his eyes widened as he spotted the Polaroid. "Woah - there's a blast from the past!" He examined the photo carefully, and then turned to Lucy. "Did you ever think about me – about *us* - all those years we were apart?"

She paused before replying. "Well, yes; I mean, you

were always there in my mind, however much I tried to forget you and move on. But I also knew that eventually – somehow - we'd end up together, whatever happened in the meantime."

Jake laughed softly. "Bet you didn't think it would be over thirty years, though, did you?"

Lucy shrugged. "Maybe not, but I tell you what I did know; that when we did meet, the sea would play a part in it…"

"Aha, so us bumping into each other that day on Brighton Pier last year wasn't a complete surprise then?"

"Not completely, no, but we've definitely come full circle now that we're back here in the beach hut." Lucy smiled.

He nodded in agreement, and then drew her closer to him. "Hey, I've an idea - how about we leave the clearing up til later? I can think of more interesting things to do, after all…"

Lucy laughed and kissed him briefly. "How did I know you'd say that?"

# 20
# CHRYSALIS

Six a.m. Dor wakes abruptly, having trained himself to do so over the past year. Anxious not to waste a second, he begins – eyes still closed - to examine his face with the tips of his fingers. Slowly. Thoroughly. Wait! He pauses for a short time over his left cheek as he feels something… something that surely wasn't there yesterday? A slight raise of the skin, a bump or coarsening - small but possibly significant: could this be it? Unable to contain his anticipation any longer, he leaps from his sleeping place and rushes over to the large mirror on the wall. Needing to know. Desperate to find out, but at the same time, afraid that, yet again, it won't be. He stares intently at his reflection. A small bluish-purple smudge meets his gaze and his shoulders slump as he recalls the unexpectedly high kick that Fren bestowed upon him yesterday. Play fighting, as brothers do. So… a bruise – nothing more.

He rests his forehead despairingly against the cool glass, closing his eyes and feeling the hopelessness wash over him like sea-froth eroding abrasions from shore-bound pebbles and shells. When is it going to happen? When is he going to finally achieve his maturity? Wistfully, he considers his friends; his acquaintances; his peers. All have gone through the process that has so far eluded Dor; some reached their maturity years ago, at ten, maybe eleven. But here he is – almost fourteen now – still with the smooth skin of a much younger being. High-pitched voice with no sign of any harsh deepening. Soft curling hair that remains resolutely on his head, showing no inclination to spread elsewhere. And, most debasing of all: delicate little fingers and toes that could easily belong to a fragile young girl, so insubstantial and dainty are they.

With a sudden flush of anger, Dor lets out an anguished groan, beating his fists impotently against the wall. It's not bloody fair! What's so wrong with him that the most natural of adolescent transformations evades him so callously? Why? He shakes his head despairingly. It can't be a genetic problem; Fren matured at the tender age of nine, throwing off the cloak of childhood almost overnight and adapting to his new semblance with confidence and aplomb. Barely turning a hair on his head – or anywhere else on his body, for that matter! Unjust!

The door opens and Dor raises his head slowly for the inevitable enquiry. His father enters, his mother close behind. "We heard a noise – is everything alright?" Tall and proud, Hal seems to depict everything that Dor himself is not. A fine specimen of maturity, confident and assertive in his form and stance. The younger male turns away, unable to bear the sight of this fully-formed being. Too soon after his daily disappointment. He mutters a reply under his breath which is hardly perceptible, even to himself. But Hal hears him; picks up on his underlying frustration. Understands. He moves closer to his son and touches him gently on the shoulder. "It will happen, you know," he comforts, his voice soft despite the amazingly low pitch. "Sometimes it just takes a little longer for some people to… change. But it will happen; it *will* come to you."

His mother comes to Dor's other side, turning his face

towards her own and examining his skin with a practised eye. For countless months she has repeated this gesture in the early morning sunlight. Probing and exploring. Expecting and hoping. Now, as always, she sighs. "You just have to be patient, son – all you can do is wait…"

But as the two of them attempt to comfort him in their usual stoic routine, Dor suddenly senses a new awareness – a slight *frisson* between his parents. He frowns, initially unsure what this is, but then, as he tunes in more acutely, recognises it as *fear;* that, despite their reassurances, they are as worried as he himself about his lack of maturity. He shudders, clammy with comprehension. Finally realises that he can't just leave his inadequacy to luck or nature any longer; he has to do something proactive to hasten the process. As his parents drift from his room, their platitudes depleted for the day, Dor knows that it is finally time to take charge of his own destiny.

Throwing himself back on the bed, he latches his fingers under his head in meditative pose. The trouble is, he doesn't have anyone close to him who has faced a similar problem. Everyone he knows seems to have practically transformed overnight, once they were within the appropriate age range. Except, of course… he thinks now of the uneasy Spectres that lurk in the shadows at the mysterious hour of 6 am. He has been aware of these non-beings ever since he was a tiny boy and even more so in the past year. He is scared of what they represent, for everyone knows why they hover during that particular time of day. They wait in hope - in desperation – aiming to take over unwary adolescent bodies in the split-second moment of transformation. They are the ones whose own bodies let them down with their inability to develop, causing them to remain indistinct and obscure; forever on the periphery. Will Dor too become one of these shapeless nonentities? Is that the reason for his parents' unease – the knowledge that soon their son will be reduced to floating around unsuspecting teenagers, trying to gain entry to a second-hand body?

"No!" Dor sits up abruptly. That will not happen to him. He needs to seek advice before it's too late; watching and waiting is not enough anymore. He makes his decision: he'll ask Fren what to do because, out of everyone he knows, his older brother is surely the one to ask…

*\*\**

"Alknosterone," Fren says sagely, glancing up from his game, smug to be acknowledged and consulted in such matters. "That's basically what initiates the transformation - it's a chemical which changes the balance of your hormones. Everyone has a certain amount of it anyway, inside the body, but during maturity, levels rise to a much higher degree and that's what stimulates the changes."

Dor breathes a sigh of relief. This seems simple enough – though maybe too simple? "So, where can I get hold of it then; can I buy it?"

Shrugging, Fren then laughs sardonically. It's an unconvincing, thin-bodied sound. "We-ll, you could, but not from any shop, no, and certainly not from a medicinal. No self-respecting doctor would allow themselves to prescribe it – it's too risky."

Dor frowns and shakes his head irritably. Then suddenly stops like a fly landing on a rotten apple. "Why? Surely if it's a natural substance – which it must be if I've got it in my body anyway – then it can't be dangerous?"

"I didn't say *dangerous*, I said *risky*," retorted Fren. He snaps his console shut with a sigh. Scratches his chin thoughtfully. "There are stories that suggest that tampering with nature is not necessarily a sensible thing to do… Apparently, it can cause side effects in some people, that sort of thing…"

"But it *does* bring on the transformation – and quickly?" Dor persists. "It does what it's supposed to?" He considers these mysterious side effects. They linger in the air like half-hearted fireflies playing at being grown-ups. But, brushing them aside, he dismisses their existence with the brashness of youth. Nothing - but nothing - could be as bad as the prospect of hovering on the side-lines of life with the faceless Spectres. It would be worth a few small side effects to finally have maturity in his grasp: it has to be!

"Yes, it's certainly supposed to hasten the process," reluctantly agrees Fren. Then narrows his eyes at his brother's determined expression. "But, seriously, is it really worth the risk? Don't you think that the process will happen naturally if you just give it a chance?"

"Give it a chance? *Give it a chance!* Don't you think I've bloody well done that?" shouts Dor, jumping up from his cross-legged position on the floor and striding over to his brother. He stops abruptly before him and shoves his face into Fren's. "Look at me – just look at me! Do you think I want to be like this for the rest of my life?"

Startled, Fren stares at him. Observes the smooth, silky skin, the cornflower blue eyes fringed with dark lashes, the pale pink hue of plump lips… He shifts uncomfortably before answering. "No… I guess you don't." Suddenly determined, he raises his head to meet Dor's eyes. Vows, unwaveringly, "Ok, I'll sort you out, bro; don't worry – I'll get you that Alknosterone if it's the last thing I do."

Dor relaxes, his slight body a spent-coil finally

allowing itself to shudder to a standstill. "Thanks Fren – I… just - thanks."

*** 

Two days later, Fren has been good to his word and Dor has in his possession the desired tablets. Normally having an open and uncomplicated relationship with their parents, Fren and Dor have had to be unusually secretive about this particular plan. Both know, with no words necessary, that Hal and Yun would be horrified at their attempt to interfere with nature. The older couple are purists of the highest form, with neither believing in even the simplest of medicines for, say, an infection or a headache. "What will be, will be," is one of Hal's much-repeated phrases. No, Dor reflects now, as he studies the unlabelled brown bottle, neither parent can be allowed any hint of what he is about to do. Ever.

Fren had been specific with his instructions when he'd shoved the plain paper bag into Dor's hands last night. "Take one a day for two days only," he'd hissed conspiratorially, darting his head this way and that, for fear of Hal or Yun stumbling upon the transaction. "You'll notice a difference during Day One and the transformation will be totally complete by the end of the second."

Dor had nodded solemnly, his hands shaking a little as he extracted the bottle from the bag, staring at the seemingly innocent container that would herald the start of his adulthood: his maturity. "Yes, ok. Thanks, Fren."

Fren had winked at him, suddenly back to his breezy self. "Hey – no worries bro. There's a few extra pills in there; we can sell them on if we come across anyone else with your problem – should be able to make a nice little profit for ourselves!" He'd then lumbered from the room, relieved that his part in the deception was over.

Now Dor carefully opens the bottle and tips out one of the tablets into the palm of his hand. Small and round, it doesn't look significant enough to bring about the transformation he so desires; can this small object *really* be his threshold to adulthood? He supposes there's only one way to find out. Glancing at his watch and observing that it's less than a minute until the optimum 6 a.m., he tips back his head and dryly gulps back the pill, closing his eyes in fervent wish as he does so. There: done!

As 6 a.m. is reached, Dor ignores the inevitable reappearance of the Spectres loitering in the periphery and hurries to his mirror, watching intently for any change in his countenance, however small. He waits. Stares. Waits some more. After a couple of hours he feels as if his eyes might fracture the glass, so great is the mesmerism between mirror and countenance. But nothing seems to have changed. Has it? Is that the fuzz of whiskery growth across his face, or just a trick of the light? He pulls the skin of his cheek to check for hair follicles. No – just a shadow. Dor bites his lip; maybe he should do something to distract himself; perhaps the changes will be forthcoming when he's not examining every pore of his face – will take him unawares, possibly.

Reluctantly, he leaves his room and goes in search of diversion. Downstairs. Yun is quietly preparing breakfast. She smiles at her younger son. "Ah Dor, I was just coming to find you; everything alright?" She peers at him searchingly.

"Fine," answers Dor. He can tell that her fingers are itching to begin the daily probing and examining and so, to deter this, he thrusts his face into her vision, showing her that he is as usual. "Nothing... yet."

She hides her disappointment well, turning to add another egg to the frying pan in a bustling, motherly fashion. "Ah well, don't worry son; tomorrow's another day."

Dor feels his hopes rise slightly at her words. Yes, another day and another pill – tomorrow would surely be both the beginning and the conclusion of his transformation. By tomorrow night, he could conceivably be a fully-fledged adult!

***

The following morning he has asked Fren to sit with him as he takes the final pill. Bleary-eyed and vague, his brother slouches on Dor's bed, watching as the younger male shakes another tablet into his hand. Again, Dor stares at the small white pill. Hesitates. "It'll work, won't it, Fren?" he questions anxiously. "This last tablet – it will make the transformation complete; it will combine with the pill from yesterday to change me?"

Fren yawns and blinks languidly at him. "Sure," he says, at length. "And if it doesn't, I'm getting my money back." He laughs, absently picking at a loose thread on Dor's blanket.

With one more nervous glance at the little white sphere, Dor again squeezes his eyes tight shut and throws back the tablet. "Work, damn you – work!" he mutters as he envisages the pill travelling unhurriedly down his body. Although tempted, today he forces himself to stay away from the mirror; to let things happen in their own good time. Slowly, he thinks; slowly throughout the day, bit by bit until this evening, when he would be totally completed.

Satisfied that his participation is over, Fren now lurches heavily from the bed and makes his way to the door. He pauses before opening it, glancing at Dor. "Going back to my room now," he mumbles indistinctly. "'K?"

Dor, having walked over to the window, is now staring outside; staring without seeing, reflecting on the power of mind over matter. He barely acknowledges his brother's exit, just giving him a distracted wave as he continues to urge his cells and molecules to do their business; to multiply and spread – to change him into what he knows he should be. It'll be soon now; very soon – he knows it!

After a short while, his concentrated fervency dissipates into impatience and he decides to make a concentrated start to the day so that the hours will pass by quickly. But, on passing his parents' bedroom door, he pauses, hearing raised voices. He frowns at the oddity of this, for very rarely do Hal and Yun argue; in fact, Dor can't remember the last time they had an altercation. He is about to move away and continue walking downstairs but suddenly hears his own name mentioned. Curious, he places an ear carefully to the door to find out more.

It's his father's voice he hears; although the older man seems to be making an attempt to keep the volume down, the frustration in his tone means that it contains a resounding quality which is difficult to ignore.

"Think about it, Yun," he's urging, his usually cheery voice now smacking of desperation. "If we don't get Dor into hiding soon, it's almost certain that he'll be seized by the Spectres. Then what'll we do? We'll be powerless to help him!"

Dor claps a hand to his mouth in dismay. *Hiding? Spectres?*

Yun's higher, softer tone interrupts. "But he will

transform soon; he has to. We just have to wait, that's all! Wait for him to change, and then he'll be safe. "

Now Hal sounds weary – despairing even. "I wish I had your confidence, I really do. But you know the situation; you examine him every day; does he really look any different now from when he was eight, nine? Is there any sign of change, seriously?"

A long silence. Eventually, Yun's voice is heard, tearful and hesitant. "N-no." Then, slightly querulously, "So, what can we do?"

"Leave it to me; I'll organise somewhere for him to go – a safe place. I'll make enquiries and get it sorted out in a day or so. The sooner the better, I'm sure you'll agree." There is a decisive tone now in his father's voice; he obviously feels better for having made this decision.

Dor stumbles away from the door. He has heard enough. Shaking, he makes his way back to his room. Locks the door behind him and sinks down onto his bed, head in hands. He isn't entirely sure which is worse; the embarrassment of having to be sent away somewhere 'safe' or the humiliation of his continued inability to transform. Oh, and not forgetting, of course, the danger of being swooped upon by the Spectres and being forced to live a non-life with them. Could things get any worse?

After a few moments, he stands and walks over to the mirror. *Please – something… anything!* But no, apart from an anxious pallor making his freckles stand out even more than usual, his cherubic round face looks just as it always does. "More's the bloody pity!" he mutters, turning away from his disloyal reflection. As he does so, however, his eyes fall on the brown bottle which is mocking him from the dressing table. He picks it up and spins it thoughtfully on the smooth surface of the table, aware of the rattle of the remaining tablets inside. His thoughts seem to spin in empathy with the small container, flickering and whirling around his brain, sparking off random emotions and ideas. "Maybe… Maybe I should just go for it and take the whole lot in one dose. What is there to lose, after all?" He starts towards the door, intending to ask Fren for his opinion, but then stops abruptly. At this stage he feels he needs to take back control of the situation. Surely making this decision and doing it alone will be a declaration of maturity; a sign to the powers that be – whoever they are - that he is ready for his transformation?

So Dor unscrews the lid and, before he can change his mind, tips the remaining tablets down his throat, not bothering to heed the quantity. *Nothing ventured, nothing gained* is his last cohesive – and somewhat clichéd - thought before he falls back onto the bed in a prolonged and dreamless sleep.

*** 

Six a.m. Dor wakes abruptly, as always. Immediately, he is aware – intuitively - that he is different; that he has finally changed. He reaches, tentatively, to his face. Yes! No longer does his skin feel soft and silky to the touch, it now has a fuzzy, calloused texture to it – the texture of adulthood! Excitedly, Dor leaps from his bed and bounds over to the mirror. *Oh, thank you, thank you!* He stares in profound admiration at his reflection; gone is the thin blond hair, the baby-blue eyes, the small and delicate features. Instead, Dor revels in the two shell-like horns protruding proudly from his skull, the black wiry hair covering his hitherto smooth complexion, the one small piercing eye positioned exactly in the middle of his forehead. Perfect – just perfect! At last: his heart's desire.

Wanting to share his newly-acquired physique, Dor

shouts out, "Hey! Fren – come here, quick!" He is fascinated by the new low pitch of his voice and tries other sounds as he waits for his brother to emerge from his pit. "Ooo! Ahh! Eee!"

Within seconds, Fren bursts into the room, a ready grin on his hirsute countenance. However, as his eye travels down Dor's body, his smile begins to fade and is progressively replaced with dismay. Then disgust. And finally: repulsion.

Dor follows his glance, swivelling the one eye to take in his lower body, and gasps, his spirits plummeting downwards at an absurd rate. Where are his fur-covered tripod limbs, able to run a mile in a matter of seconds? Where is his magnificent scaled tail, powerful enough to flick the most persistent of birds from the trees with a single quiver? Where – and now he feels the shameful tears, warm and betraying, trickling down his face – where is his muscular upper body with scales that can't be penetrated by any man or any beast? Conspicuous by their absence, that's where. All he has below his neck, he realises in a mixture of terror and despair, is an undistinguishable and almost ethereal type of... *froth*. He steels himself to touch his lower body – to check that this has really happened - but recoils as his touch meets nothing but insubstantiality: all that is there is a sensation – just the slightest sensation.

Dor forces himself to raise his head and face his brother. Eye meets eye. Horns glint on horns. Bile rising in his throat, Fren turns abruptly on his hooves. Appalled. Sickened. He spits out just the one word over his shoulder as he charges from the room to fetch their parents. "Mutant!"

# 21
# SHUTDOWN

Grace sighed as the wailing started up next door. The baby again - all it had done was cry since she had heard them move in last week. Grabbing the TV remote, she stabbed at the volume button. The presenter's voice began to fill the room until the bawling was relatively muted in comparison. There; that was better. She shouldn't have to put up with that sort of caterwauling – not at her age.

Kayla sighed as Toby continued to howl. Rocked him gently, backwards and forwards. "Come on, Tobes, don't cry – *please* - it'll be o-" She jerked her head up in shock as the TV volume next door was suddenly amplified. Now she could hear every effing, every blinding as 'that bastard Joe' found out that, despite all his denials, he *was* indeed the father. Close to tears, Kayla buried her face into Toby's soft hair, desperately trying to stop her anxiety from overwhelming her.

\*\*\*

Without warning, the lights first flickered and then completely extinguished. As the room was plunged into darkness, Grace gasped, spilling drops of her tea painfully into her lap. Exclaimed aloud, "Oh!" She stood up, brushing down her skirt. Then stumbled slowly to the door. Opened it and peered out…

As the room suddenly darkened, Kayla gasped, clutching the now-sleeping Toby closer to her. What now? Rising carefully, she hoisted the little boy onto her hip and felt her way, one-handed to where she thought the front door would be. Fumbled for the handle, eventually finding and pressing it down. Stared out into the blackness of the communal corridor...

In the darkness, the two women paused, silhouettely framed in their respective doorways. Only the heavy breathing of the baby punctuated the silence – a constant which seemed to bridge their uncertainty a little. Somehow. Grace cleared her throat and then spoke quickly, as if anxious to get any interaction over and done with. "Probably just a power cut."

Kayla shifted Toby to a more comfortable position on her hip. When she replied, her voice was quieter, reluctant to scratch the smooth canvas of the darkness. "H-has it happened before?"

Grace hesitated. "Well, no, but... old building, lots of tenants – bound to create an overload eventually, I suppose."

Nodding, Kayla then remembered that she couldn't be seen. "Right. So we just have to wait for it to be sorted?"

Although the girl's words were expressed confidently enough, Grace heard something in her tone that - when she thought about it afterwards - she would've missed if it hadn't been dark. Something which seemed to touch her. She surprised herself with her next words. "If you like, you could come inside with me; we could wait together for the electricity to come back on?"

Kayla faltered, pondering the correlation between this seemingly inoffensive question and the angry pounding - an umbrella? – on the dividing wall when Toby had been at his most fractious. The two didn't seem to sit well together. "I – I'm not sure..."

Grace didn't know why, but she sensed it was

important to get the girl to join her. "I've got some candles stashed away somewhere – it would be better than sitting here in the dark?"

Kayla thought of Toby's fright if he were to wake up to total darkness. The screaming. The shuddering. There was no choice, really. She sighed, almost imperceptibly. "Ok - thanks."

***

Once settled in Grace's small flat, candles flickering gently on the coffee table in front of them, the two women looked across at each other. Each gave a half-smile. At each other. At the situation.

Now lowering her eyes, Grace turned instead to the sleeping baby. Gently touched his hair. "He - he looks a little like…" she began. Stopped.

Kayla raised her gaze to the older woman's. "Like?"

After taking a breath, Grace spoke so softly that Kayla had to strain to hear her. "I had a baby myself, back in the sixties. Same colour hair as…?"

"Toby," prompted Kayla, nodding as she watched Grace's face soften in the candlelight.

"Toby. But my baby died; he contracted pneumonia soon after his father and I split up." Grace sighed and looked back down into the tiny flicker of light. "He – Joseph - was only two."

"That's awful – really terrible." Kayla gasped. She clutched Toby tighter.

Grace nodded. "Take good care of your little one, won't you?"

"I will. Always." Kayla bit her lip and, emboldened by Grace's secret, seemed to reach a decision. "He's not mine, though – he's my sister's little boy."

"Oh?" Grace was puzzled. "But you're… looking after

him for her?"

"Yes. She's not well, you see; she's been in a… psychiatric unit, for the past year and a half – I've had Toby with me since he was born."

Grace raised her eyebrows. "That's quite an undertaking for a young woman."

Kayla's voice was matter of fact. "Not really. She'd have done the same for me if it was the other way round. We visit her weekly so she can see Toby." She frowned. "Though it'll be harder now we've left the hostel – it was practically down the road from the unit, you see. Now we're miles further away."

There was a few moments of silence while both women gazed into the candlelight. Eventually Grace spoke. "I have a little car," she began. "Maybe I could give you a lift each week?"

Slowly, Kayla's face lit up and she smiled. "That would be great, if you don't mind. I know there's buses and all but, well, it's hard with a baby."

Grace nodded. "It's sorted then."

"Thank you, I'd be really grateful. And… if there's anything you'd like me to do for you?" Kayla wasn't sure what she could possibly offer the old lady, but she wanted this new … *arrangement?* to be on an equal footing.

About to refuse, purely out of habit, Grace suddenly understood. She reflected, taking a breath. "Perhaps… you could keep me company now and again – you *and* Toby? That's what I'd like."

Kayla nodded. The two of them smiled at each other, just as the lights flickered back on.

# 22
# RED TELEPHONE BOX

The muddy ground is a sludge of security that Joe welcomes. Dull, slushy, predictable - it is completely tolerable. Undemanding. Perfect for his state of mind. His *now*. Anything more - or less - wouldn't be right. So he keeps his head down and his eyes half-shuttered as he wanders along the country lanes, not thinking about anything beyond the satisfying sensation of Wellington boot on slush. *Squelch.*

It is part of the daily routine, his morning walk. Walking. *Just* walking, but that's acceptable; it's a physical activity which doesn't need thought or response. It just *is*. For the past few months, this walk has shaped the major part of Joe's day. It could be seen as an interlude between the sun rising and setting. The daily pound of his footsteps play out a satisfying rhythm that neatly postpones thoughts that he knows will have to be addressed at some stage. But not yet. He's not ready.

As he approaches the familiar uneven clearing that marks mid-way, Joe raises his head to make the daily decision - *left or right?* - but then stops, confused. A little way away, possibly seven or eight metres, stands a large object that definitely wasn't there yesterday. A red telephone box. Strange. He furrows his brows slightly in an attempt to collate his thoughts and make sense of this new development but then, overwhelmed, decides that it may just be easier to go over and have a look. He wanders towards the booth, slowing his pace as recollections come to the surface of his consciousness...

*A red telephone box.* He hasn't seen one since... well, he supposes it was since he was a small boy, growing up in the depths of Croydon. Years ago. But telephone boxes have always held a fascination for him, for there's something about the structure, the colour, the cohesion, that makes him feel... reassured. He nods his head slightly, acknowledging finding the right word. *Reassured.*

Joe remembers the very first time he'd carefully heaved open the red, glass-panelled door and entered into the small enclosure that was the telephone box. He must have been about seven or eight or so, on a mission from Mum to invite Nan to tea. Nan had a phone in her living room at home, but Joe's parents didn't. Not yet. For Joe, using a public telephone was an occasion; a privilege. His hand clammy as he clutched the 10p coin, he had felt the butterflies in his tummy perform a little dance all of their own in the excitement and responsibility of this new experience. But once inside the kiosk, he'd felt protected. Cocooned. Despite the faint aroma of what he later realised was a combination of Eau de Urinal and damp, he'd picked up the heavy black receiver with confidence, ignoring the years of ear-grime, and dialled the number. Slowly and carefully. Waited. It had occurred to him as he gazed around with curiosity at the business cards and scrawled numbers plastering the inside of the cubicle, that this was a place of mystery – almost like another world...

That had been the start of his absorption with telephone boxes. Fascinated, he had sought them out in whichever village or town he and his parents visited, drawing irregular sketches of their different features (for they *were* all different, he discovered). He even, for he was that sort of child, made it his quest to find out facts about each box, noting them down in a small spiral-bound notepad... *designed by Sir George Gilbert Scott... introduced in London during 1925... only 1000 produced initially...* Specifics which were important to him. Then.

*Obsessed,* Joe thinks now, smiling a little at the thought of the scabby-kneed boy from that time. That was the word he would have used then, had he known it: obsessed. Just like all those train spotters and anorak-clad bird watchers that are the butt of jokes and derision across the land. He shakes his head. Telephone boxes! But... he has to admit that they still hold an interest for him even now, more than twenty years later; it may be repressed, true enough, but it's still in evidence. Most notably with the subtle – and not so subtle - inclusion of telephone boxes in every one of his novels. When he was still working, of course.

He reaches the booth and stands in front of it, just looking. And as he looks, one of his Nan's old favourite phrases drifts into his mind, comfortingly familiar from his childhood: *they don't make 'em like they used to.* It occurs to Joe that nowhere better would this apply than to red telephone boxes. Particularly this one. It is safe to say that it is a real beauty. It stands – he estimates – over eight feet tall, resplendently shiny and fresh, considering its probable age. Peering at the scroll-like 'TELEPHONE' sign situated on the white roof - which boasts black writing on white background, a metal filial in the middle and four swirls at the corners – Joe frowns, flickers of recollection infiltrating his brain, nudging him into recollections from his boyhood research. Because this particular model is special, different. Surely it's an original K1 box? Yes - it has to be. None of the later boxes had this particular attention to detail. He peers round the side of the box, noting with satisfaction that it has alternating white and red sides, each displaying eight glass panels. Definitely the K1!

After his initial animation, Joe then bites his lip, finding it absurdly difficult to make the simple decision as to what to do next. Will he go into the box and investigate further, or just continue on his walk? *On* would be easier, with no further interruption to his lethargy, but… unusually, he considers the more complex alternative of *in*. For a tiny speck of interest has started to develop in the dusty corners of his curiosity… Right. Before he changes his mind, he grasps hold of the cold metal handle and pulls the heavy door open, stepping inside. He stares around in amazement – it actually *is* one of the originals *and* in pristine condition too! Containing an ashtray, writing desk, notepad and mirror, the whole interior is an exact and meticulous preservation of time. He touches each object gently – reverently even – admiring the precision of its design, understanding, possibly for the first instance in his life, the yearning of many older folk for the bygone years. Craftsmanship. Simplicity.

Intrigued, Joe now stretches his fingers towards the black Bakelite handset, gently lifting the receiver from its cradle and positioning it to his ear. He is surprised to hear not a ringtone - or even a dull vacuum - but soft breathing. "Yes," he says – somehow needing no question or exclamation mark to punctuate the monotone. As he speaks, it strikes him that he is acquiescing to a potentially awkward situation - one which he would normally avoid. A situation which could easily be resolved by his hanging up the receiver and continuing on his way. But he doesn't. For today is different. Somehow.

"Joe." The voice that replies is gentle and familiar – heart-rendingly familiar. Joe gasps out of inertia, almost dropping the hand piece, in his incomprehension of what is happening. *Beth? How...?* Her voice continues, the tone quiet and caring. "I know this is hard to understand - I don't even know myself how it was allowed to happen, but I do know that we have only a very short time. Just minutes. So I need you to listen."

Joe nods, speechless, before remembering that she can't see him, then speaks up, this time his voice a wavering mixture of hope and doubt. "Yes...?"

"Joe; don't blame yourself for the accident. It wasn't anyone's fault – it was exactly that: an accident. It was my time, I know that now. But it's not yours. *You* need to start moving on; go back to what you used to love and begin again. It will distract you. Get easier in time. We'll be together eventually; *always* remember that. Remember, Joe." Her voice grows fainter on his name as a fizz of static resounds and then is replaced by stillness. Silence.

Joe continues to cradle the phone with both hands and closes his eyes. For months, he has longed to hear Beth's voice. This is a gift more precious than any other he could imagine receiving. A gift which shouldn't be wasted. He slowly replaces the receiver. Takes a deep breath. Leaves the telephone box.

As he retraces his steps back along the path, Beth's words resound over and over in his mind: *go back to what you used to love doing... go back to what you used to love doing...* He considers her words carefully. Thought about his writing. Once his hobby, then eventually his job, mainly due to Beth's encouragement and support. Can he go back to writing? It *is* possible in theory, he supposes, but he thinks it unlikely that the passion and fire he once had is still there. Not now.

Joe walks a little further, deep in thought. Realises that this is the first real mental reflection he has allowed himself for months. *Writing*. He *could* do it, he supposes. Yes, he would be rusty at first, but trying again would give him something new to focus on – something to work towards. Yes. Unaware to anyone but the non-curious sparrows occasionally dotting the path in front of him, his shoulders raise slightly, and the set of his jaw becomes a little more determined as he considers the implications of Beth's words.

Looking back towards the red telephone box – for closure? – Joe is only faintly surprised to see that it is no longer there. He nods to himself: yes. *Quid pro quo.*

# ABOUT THE AUTHOR

Vanessa J. Horn lives in Havant, Hampshire and has been writing since 2012, when she took a sabbatical year out from her teaching career. She now alternates her working days between teaching and writing, which is the ideal situation, in her view.

She has been published in literary magazines such as Bella Mused and has won short story competitions including Word Hut, Cazart, Berkhamsted and Thynks Publications.

She enjoys playing piano and flute and has a degree from the Royal College of Music in London. Two of the stories in the collection reflect on how music can shape or define a character's life, sometimes to detrimental effect. She also loves going to the theatre and cinema with friends and family, and investigating new cafes for coffee and cake.

Most of the inspirations for Vanessa's stories come from everyday situations and scenarios that she encounters and experiences, often retold with a large helping of artistic licence, particularly those dealing with the afterlife! She is a self-confessed people watcher; she is interested in what motivates and impels people to do what they do, especially when those actions are bound to have far-reaching or even devastating consequences. The 'what ifs' of life interest her enormously and form a basis of many of the stories in this collection.

# OTHER BOOKS FROM ALFIE DOG FICTION

## Short Story Collections

3am and Wide Awake - Sarah England
A Wish for Christmas – The Christmas Collection
Bedtime Stories to Remember – children's stories from
Patricia Boulton
Blue's Adventures – Maggie Jones
By My Side – Romance Collection
Came as 'Me', Left as 'We' – Women's Fiction
Cobweb Capers – Children's stories from Dr J. E. McGee
Essence of Humour – The Humour Collection
Home Sweet Home – children's stories from Joan
Zambelli
Love, Laughter, Tears – Hilary Halliwell
On the Changi Beat, 1961 – 1962 – Terence Brand
Read it Again – Children's Collection
Six Stupid Sheep and Other Yarns – Susan Wright
Stuffed Robins Don't Fly – Gill McKinlay
Sweet Talk – Samantha Tonge
The Day Death Wore Boots – Ghost Story Collection
The Ghostly Victorians – Annette Siketa
This Land is My Land – Action and Adventure
Thrice Upon a Time – Fairytale Collection
Up The Garden Path – Patsy Collins

**Novels**
Alfie's Woods – Rosemary J. Kind
Double Take – Annette Siketa
In the Kitchen with a Knife – Susan Wright
The Appearance of Truth – Rosemary J. Kind
The Ghosts of Camals College – Teen fiction from Annette Siketa
The Lifetracer – Rosemary J. Kind
The Sound of Pirates – Terence Brand
The Summer Boy – Henry Mitchell

# Alfie Dog Fiction

*Taking your imagination for a walk*

For hundreds of short stories, collections
and novels visit our website at
www.alfiedog.com

Join us on Facebook
http://www.facebook.com/AlfieDogLimited

Printed in Great Britain
by Amazon.co.uk, Ltd.,
Marston Gate.